WICKED WHITE

MICHELLE A. VALENTINE

Published by Montlake Romance, Seattle

www.apub.com

Amazon, the Amazon logo, and Montlake are trademarks of Amazon.com, Inc., or its affiliates.

ISBN-13: 9781477830956
ISBN-10: 1477830952

Cover design by Letitia Hasser

Printed in the United States of America

To Brian, thank you

Chapter 1

ACE

This place is a fucking circus. Sure, on the outside it may appear to be a well-oiled machine, but to someone who lives it every day, the music business is a crazy ride.

My band is headlining Summerfest tonight. One of the biggest music festivals in America, held in Milwaukee, Wisconsin, for eleven straight days. It's pure insanity here.

I sit on display like a monkey in a cage under a white-topped tent in the blazing ninety-degree weather while a line of fans as far as the eye can see wait to get my signature. I'll give the fans one thing—they're dedicated, because this heat is miserable.

Jane Ann, my road manager, hovers behind me as the fans come through one by one to get their thirty seconds with me while I sign whatever crap they just bought from the merchandise booth with my band's name on it, Wicked White. I hate it when she does that—monitors my behavior. It's times like these when she's a thorn in my side. If she wasn't so damn good at her job, and the reason the band gained the notoriety it has, I'd tell her to take a hike.

"Ohmygod! Ace, I love you," the busty blond wearing a too-tight tank top squeals as she approaches my table. "Will you sign my chest?"

I fight the urge hard to not roll my eyes at this chick. This is the part of my job that I absolutely loathe—signing another human being's skin. Most of these women have no shame and will flop their tit out on a dime for the thrill of me touching it with a Sharpie. It kills me that I can't refuse. Jane Ann has made it perfectly clear to me what my role is as a rock star—I'm to smile and sign whatever they ask me to.

"Never refuse a fan. The media is everywhere. One negative video posted to the Internet can ruin your career and the brand we've worked so hard to create for Wicked White," Jane Ann told me last time I complained.

As much as it pains me, I smile at the blond and wave her in closer. "Sure, babe. Just point to the spot."

The woman giggles and her friends shove her forward, almost daring her to approach me. She grabs the front of her shirt and yanks one side down along with her bra, far enough that half of her nipple is exposed. She runs a finger slowly over the mounded flesh and licks her lips. "Right here."

I know it's an act of seduction, and on most men I'm sure this would get the girl noticed, possibly gaining her backstage entrance from a horny motherfucker looking to score with a groupie. That shit don't work on me, though. I want a nice girl. Someone who I could take home to a mother—if I had one.

The groupie sighs happily as I etch my name with a black Sharpie across her warm skin. It's completely illegible, but that's irrelevant considering she'll more than likely sweat it off before the day's end.

The rest of her friends, following suit, have me sign their bodies in different places as well.

"After these three, wrap it up. We've got to get Ace backstage," Jane Ann tells the guy in the yellow security shirt standing next to my table.

Great. Nothing like pissing off a couple hundred fans after they stood in line for an hour to meet me.

Jane Ann needs to implement the ticket idea that I suggested earlier this year, but I know she'll never do it. Limiting tickets limits merch sales, and there's no way she won't squeeze out every penny that she can, so that's out.

After I finish with the last woman, the guard says, "All right, folks, Ace has to go."

A collective sound of boos flows through the air as I stand and turn away from the table. Jane Ann waits for me with her flaming red hair tossed casually over her shoulder. The bright red leather pants she's wearing are about two sizes too small, and the low-cut blouse shows entirely too much skin, but that's her normal, everyday gear. She threads her arm through mine and stares up at me with her blue eyes as she leads me out of the tent toward the backstage area. "The women are really starting to take notice of you, Ace. You're well on your way to becoming a true sex symbol. Soon Ace White will be a household name."

I shake my head, not caring a bit if the world knows the stage name the record label gave me. "I could give a shit about that. You know all I care about is the music. Speaking of . . . did you tell the label I plan on writing the songs for the next record?"

She sighs and rolls her eyes. "I did, Ace, but you know how the bigwigs are. They want to make sure the songs appeal to the mass market, so they want to bring in the same producers you worked with on the last album. Johnny Moses has some terrific songs picked out that really fit your voice."

I pull back, halting her in place. "Hold up. You've heard the writers' demos already and didn't send them to me?"

"You've just been so busy making appearances that I figured you wouldn't have time and would be happy with what I chose. Don't you trust my judgment anymore?" She raises a perfectly manicured eyebrow. "Remember, it was me helping you change your style that took you to this new platform. This is the level we've been dying to get to."

I shake my head, my dark hair falling into my eyes. "My music would've eventually gotten me there."

She pats my chest as a look of pity crosses her face. "Keep telling yourself that if it makes you feel better, but we both know it was me and the choices I made for you that pushed you to this level, not those sad little acoustic songs you sang to bar crowds of twenty people. This is the big leagues, kid. You'd do best not to throw a fit over something as simple as a song choice. You need to give the fans what they've grown to expect from you. They're what bring in the money. Trust me."

This should shock me, her treating me like a puppet on the string that she controls, but it doesn't. It's true that over the last two years since she discovered me, Jane Ann has morphed me into a million-dollar singer. Fronting a band that Mopar Records created should've been a dream job, but it's not. I don't get to sing any of the music that I enjoy singing—and writing? Forget it. The label won't trust me with creative liberties one bit.

That's what pisses me off the most.

I'm an artist. I don't want to keep re-creating someone else's vision for my entire career. I want to be free to express myself and control my own success or failure by allowing the fans to hear my original songs, not ones I'm forced to sing.

But it's been made very clear to me by Jane Ann time and time again that if I want to continue to have label backing, I have to play what they give me until the record label says otherwise.

I know she's patronizing me, but if I don't want to lose everything I've worked for, I have to go along.

For now.

"All right, but can I at least listen to the new songs I'll be recording?" I ask, completely deflated.

A satisfied smile pours over her face. She's clearly delighted I'm giving in. "Of course, darling. After tonight's show I'll play them for you."

Once upon a time I believed this woman was actually my friend. But that was before the piles of cash were rolling in and I became her primary source of income. She told me our friendship didn't have anything to do with money.

Having friends has never been one of my strong suits in my last twenty-six years, so I desperately wanted to believe that Jane Ann was someone I could actually trust. She seemed genuinely to have my best interests at heart regarding my music career when I first met her, but now I'm not so sure that she does.

It was lonely growing up as a foster child, bouncing from place to place—never really having a steady home. I never had time to make friends, not real ones anyway. That's what led me to music. It was the one constant in my life. The one thing no one could ever take away from me. I spent most of my youth alone in my room, learning to play every instrument known to man. Focusing on something other than the fact that my real mother didn't want me anymore seemed to keep me out of trouble.

I walk next to Jane Ann as we wind our way through the maze of roadies and stagehands working to get everything ready for Wicked White's set. "Are the rest of the guys here?"

"Yes. Already warmed up and ready. They were waiting until you were done with your autograph session to go over tonight's set list with you."

"Good," I say. "I hate when they're late and we have to go round them up."

"I've spoken with them about their tardiness and explained just because they were the best the studio could find for the job doesn't mean they aren't replaceable. Everyone is replaceable."

Even me is what I'm dying to say, but know that she'd just laugh and yet deny it. Jane Ann is a label talent scout but has put that position on hold to be my tour manager since this is my first major tour and I have issues with trusting random strangers. Jane Ann also gets a percentage of all my money like an agent would. Last year alone Wicked White grossed over six million dollars from the tour, not counting any of the money made on music downloads and miscellaneous shit that got sold with the band name on it.

Wicked White is not a real band, but a product.

The cell in my back pocket buzzes with the alert of an incoming call, so I grab it and check the screen.

The name that flashes isn't one that I've seen in a long time, but it's always nice to hear from the one person that I actually care about.

I pull away from Jane Ann. "Excuse me. I have to take this."

After I take a couple steps, I press the green button. "Hey, Mom. How are you?"

"Ace Johnson?" The deep voice on the other end is one that I don't recognize. It puzzles me how this strange man knows my real name, and why is he calling from my foster mother's home number?

"Yes. Do I know you?"

"No. I'm afraid not. I'm Officer Butler with the Franklin County Sheriff's Department, and I'm afraid that I have some upsetting news. Ms. Sarah Johnson was found in her home unresponsive moments ago. She's been transferred to Grant Medical Center in critical condition. As you're listed as her son in her address book, we thought you would like to be notified." His tone is very businesslike as he rattles off the specifics on where the hospital is located, but I'm barely registering what he's saying.

I swallow hard as I'm faced with the hard reality that the one person in the world that gives a shit about me may not make it. I need to be with her. I have to get there. Now. "Thank you, Officer. I'm on my way."

When I end the call, I stuff my phone into my back pocket and turn to find Jane Ann staring at me with narrowed eyes. "Where exactly are you on your way to?"

I square my shoulders. I know she's not going to like what I have to say, but it doesn't matter. Not Jane Ann, or anyone else for that matter, is going to stand in my way of getting to Mom. "My mother is sick. She needs me."

I turn in the opposite direction of the stage, but Jane Ann is quick to follow on my heels. "You can't leave now!"

"Watch me," I say.

"Ace, wait!" Jane Ann grabs my arm and jumps in front of me to halt me from going any farther. "Let's think reasonably. You're on tour. There are fifteen thousand people out in that crowd tonight that have paid their hard-earned money to see you. Just go out and do the show, then we'll talk about you driving to Ohio tonight. You can't make the fans suffer. It will kill your career if you stand them up."

I pinch the bridge of my nose. A huge part of me wants to tell her to fuck off and just go, but there's a part that hates the idea of losing my career. I've worked so hard to get to where I'm at, so I'm torn.

After a few moments of debate, I sigh, deciding that I can just jet after our set. "Fine. Let's get this show on the road."

Jane Ann smiles, her white teeth sparkling, when she's figured out that she's gotten her way. "You're making the right decision, Ace."

Anger boils within me that I'm stuck here, unable to leave like I want for fear of what I'd lose.

Jane Ann hooks her arm through mine and leads me toward the stage again. Once we make it to where the rest of the guys in my band are standing around waiting to take the stage, they all glance up in my direction. The guys have on their standard 100 percent white stage attire, a corny gimmick Jane Ann thought would be good as our signature look on stage.

JJ's blue eyes meet mine, and then he quickly glances in the opposite direction. He always looks pissed off. The dark hair and tan complexion he has just increase his menacing appearance. JJ Kraft, known as JJ White to the world—another ridiculous demand by the label for us to all use White as our last names on stage—is the lead guitarist for Wicked White, but that job isn't the one he really wants. It's been difficult becoming a cohesive unit with the guys in the band, namely because we never knew each other before the label slapped us all together and told us if we wanted a deal, we needed to get along and be professional. Money and fame are two things that are difficult for any band to struggle with once they come their way, but it's even harder when you have no personal connection with one another.

JJ has always had his eye on my job. He wants to be the front man so bad he can taste it, and I guess having to follow my lead is enough to set him off every damn day. It's like he's just biding his time, waiting for me to screw up so he can jump in and take my spot.

"I'm glad all you guys are here on time," Jane Ann addresses the band as we stand in a circle. "I see my little warning of imposing fines for tardiness has made a difference."

"Not all of us have you as our personal fucking wristwatch," Tyler, our drummer, answers snidely, a piece of his dirty-blond hair falling into his eyes. "Why don't the rest of us get the same coddling that Ace gets? You always take it easy on him."

Luke, our redheaded bass player, laughs beside him, obviously in total agreement that I'm babied.

I could try to defend myself—tell these guys to fuck off because I don't get any special treatment, but I can't. I know I get treated differently. Time and time again when I ask Jane Ann to stop making a fuss over just me all the time, she tells me that I'm the true talent of this band—the rest of the guys are a dime a dozen. But me, I'm the star—the one people pay good money to see.

"So what's our set list like for tonight, Your Highness?" JJ asks mockingly.

My nostrils flare as I attempt to rein in my already boiling anger. "Same set as last night, but we'll be canceling the next couple of shows on the tour."

"What?!" Jane Ann and JJ ask in unison.

I flinch, completely flustered as to why Jane Ann acts like this is news to her. We just talked about me leaving a few minutes ago, so this shouldn't shock her. Now JJ, on the other hand, I knew he'd be pissed. If we don't play the dates booked, we don't get paid.

"What the fuck do you mean we're canceling?" Luke asks, his fiery tone matching the color of his hair. "We've booked enough dates to be set for a long time. We can't go canceling shit now."

"Look, guys, I'm sorry, but my mother is sick—"

"That's horseshit. You don't even have a mother. You were a fucking orphan."

"Shut your damn mouth before I shut it for you," I fire back.

JJ takes a step closer to me. "That sounds like a threat."

"You bet your ass it was."

9

My pulse races under my skin as JJ and I stand almost toe to toe while we stare each other down. I've got him by at least two inches with my six-foot frame, but he's got about sixty pounds on me. He's a gym rat, where I pride myself on speed and agility with running.

I don't like to fight. It goes against the mellow life I want to lead, but I'm not afraid to defend myself or anyone else that may need my help.

Jane Ann wedges her small body between us when she sees that neither of us plans on backing down anytime soon. "Both of you knock this shit off right now. I won't tolerate physical violence of any kind. This isn't going to happen if you want to stay on Mopar's payroll."

JJ takes a step back and raises his hands in surrender. "Fine. Just keep Boy Wonder here out of my face."

I tense and begin to lunge forward, but Jane Ann's hand on my chest stops me. "Cool it, Ace. This is neither the time nor place." She turns to the rest of the guys. "You three, go wait side stage."

I take a deep breath and blow it out through pursed lips as the guys walk away from me. Never did I imagine a music career being this full of utter bullshit. Not only do I constantly have Jane Ann up my ass about doing what's best for Wicked White, but the label and the band love to jump on me every chance they get.

I fucking hate it.

I wish I'd never signed that deal.

I wish I still played to small crowds and lived in the land of obscurity.

Jane Ann whips her head back in my direction. "What in the hell were you thinking telling them you're canceling shows? You don't have that kind of authority."

"But you just said that I could go after the show tonight," I argue. "Why wouldn't I tell them I'll be gone for a couple days?"

She shakes her head. "I never said that you could go. Do you know how much money we'll lose if you don't show up at those next two shows? You aren't going anywhere."

I open my mouth to protest, but Jane Ann begins shoving me in the direction of the stage the moment Wicked White's name is announced. "Now get out there."

Flabbergasted and almost in a dreamlike state, I allow her to keep pushing me until I've got one foot on the stage. Tyler, Luke, and JJ begin playing the first song in our set list, and I stare at Jane Ann.

This woman isn't my friend.

I turn and take in the faces of each of my bandmates one by one. None of them are my friends. They could give a shit less about me. I just told them my mother is sick and they all blow me off like my feelings don't matter.

I thread my fingers into my bronze hair as it hits me hard. I hate these people just as much as they hate me, and I can't be around them for one more second. I don't care what I'm losing. It's nothing compared with my sanity and the self-worth I'll lose by sticking around and continuing to be used.

To make sure they get my message above the deafening music that's playing around the outdoor stage, I raise both of my hands to the guys and flip them the middle finger before I storm off stage.

2

ACE

I stare at Mom lying in the hospital bed before me. Her hair has grayed even more than the last time I saw her, and the wrinkles around her eyes have deepened. I pull the chair up next to her and take a seat before holding her hand, careful not to disturb any of the tubes hooked to the IV in her vein. Her hand is cold, much colder than what it should feel like. There's a white plastic tube coming from her mouth, and it's hooked to a machine that forces air into her lungs.

Fuck. She doesn't look good. The fact that she's not woken up since they found her unresponsive yesterday scares the shit out of me. I don't really remember my real mother. The state of Ohio took me away from her when I was six, and I bounced from home to home until I was twelve. No one wanted to adopt a little kid riddled with the damage a neglectful mother inflicted. It wasn't until the state placed me with Sarah that I found a permanent home. She was the only person who took the time to get to know me. The only one who helped me overcome the coldness of the world by showing me that love did exist, because *she* loved me. She was the only one.

I wish I could help her—that I could take her pain away somehow like she did mine.

I thread my fingers into my hair and shove it out of my face. I've never liked my hair long, but Jane Ann insists that the long, golden-brown locks, along with my beard, are my signature look. She told me to never change it.

A graying-haired nurse with a few fine lines around her eyes walks into the room and checks all the machines, and then she turns her gaze on me. She frowns, and the sadness touches her eyes, making her pity for me evident.

"Are you her son?" she asks.

I nod, wearing that label proudly. "Yeah, I am."

"They told me that you were notified. Did you contact the rest of her family?"

I shake my head. "She doesn't have any. She was an orphan, so it's just me."

She grabs the other chair in the room and pulls it up next to mine. "I'm Joelle. This is the second twelve-hour shift I've spent taking care of your mother. She's a fighter, but I'm afraid things don't look so good. From the report I received, she was able to phone nine-one-one but wasn't able to talk to the operator who answered. They're figuring from that time until the paramedics arrived it was close to twelve minutes. We think she lost consciousness right after she made that call, which is a long time for the brain to be without oxygen, so the odds are really stacked against her."

I take a deep breath and blow it out slowly through pursed lips. "What happened to her, exactly?"

"Her dialysis port ruptured open and she bled out. She attempted to stop the bleeding, but it was so much so fast there was no way she could stop it on her own. We gave her a transfusion after she was revived in the emergency room."

Tears burn my eyes before they leak out and spill down my cheeks. Joelle rubs my back in that caring way a mother sometimes does to comfort a child.

I wish I could've been there. I'll never be able to tell her how much I loved her and how much she meant to me, and that I would've never amounted to anything if she hadn't encouraged my love of music.

"It's hard, I know," Joelle says. "Tell her how you feel. Tell her that you love her. They say that the hearing is the last thing to go. I think she's been holding on to see you before she goes. Say your good-byes and let her know that it's okay if she wants to go because you know how much pain she's in."

Joelle pats my shoulder and stands, leaving me alone with Sarah again in the room. The constant beeps and rhythmic sounds of the ventilator are the only sounds in the room. I stare at Mom, lying there so frail, and begin crying even harder.

How am I supposed to say good-bye to someone who means so much to me? I took it for granted that I could come back here and see her whenever I wanted, and now it's too late. This is it, and it's not fair.

I adjust in my seat and grip her hand in both of mine. "Mom . . ." My voice cracks as I attempt to speak. "I'm sorry it took me so long to get here. I should've been here to tell you . . . to make sure you knew how much I love you. You're the only person in my life who's ever cared for me, and that means more to me than you'll ever know."

I take a deep breath as tears continue to stream down my face. "I wish you would wake up. I need you to wake up, and that's terribly selfish because the nurse told me how damaged your body is and that you're probably in a lot of pain, but I love you, Mom. I just need you to know that, and as much as it kills me, it's okay for you to go."

A sob tears through my chest. "It's okay to let go."

Almost as if on cue, there's a small twitch in her hand, like she's trying to tell me that she's heard me before the machines attached to her start going crazy with all kinds of alarms.

I jump up, fear coursing through every part of me. "Mom? *Mom?!* Someone help me!"

Nurse Joelle rushes into the room, shouting orders at the team of people behind her. "Someone get a doctor in here stat! She's coding!"

"Code blue: ICU room two oh three four," the overhead announces to the entire hospital.

A short woman wearing scrubs pushes herself between the bed and me. "Sir, we're going to need you to step out of the room. Sir. Sir!"

I hear the woman, but it's like I'm in a foggy haze, watching the people swarm around Mom. One tall man begins doing chest compressions as another injects a needle into the IV tubing.

When the small woman shoves me out into the hallway, she closes the door in my face. My hands instantly grip handfuls of my hair as I begin to pace and freak the fuck out.

This isn't right! It's not her time.

I stare up at the white-tiled ceiling, wishing I could see through it to heaven so I could reason with God to allow Mom to stay. She's the best person I know and she belongs here. He has enough fucking angels already. He doesn't need to take mine.

I'm not ready for this!

I know I told her it was okay for her to go, but I didn't mean it. I want to rush back in there and beg her selfishly to stay. For me.

After twenty minutes of waiting outside the door for some answers, not one person coming or going from Mom's room willing to talk to me, the commotion inside the room dies down.

A man in a white lab coat emerges from the room, followed by Joelle, both appearing very tired with frowns on their faces when they find me standing there. I know from the expression on Joelle's face the news she has to tell me is information that I don't want to hear—that will bring my world crashing down.

"Son . . ." the man starts to say, but I close my eyes, wishing he won't allow the words to leave his lips.

I shake my head as I back slowly away from them. "No. *No!*"

"I'm sorry," Joelle says. "We did everything we could."

I claw at my chest as it begins caving in, breaking my heart in the process. There's no air. I can't breathe. It's all too much.

Joelle puts her hand on my shoulder as I slump against the cold brick wall, needing it to hold me up. "This isn't easy, I know, but if you want to see her . . ."

Tears roll down my face as I attempt to breathe and not pass out right here on the spot. Everything around me fucking closes in and I continue to gasp for air.

"Do you want to go in there? It's okay if you don't."

I nod. "I want to see her."

Joelle leads me into the room. It's hard staring at Mom's lifeless body, knowing that it's merely a shell, and that her spirit is long gone.

"Give him a minute," Joelle instructs everyone in the room, and they clear out. When we're alone, she turns to me. "Take your time."

The silence is deafening the moment the door closes behind the nurse. I take a deep breath and use the back of my hand to wipe my tears away. It's no use. The tears keep falling and I'm powerless to stop them.

I bend down and wrap my arms around Mom's frail shoulders, burying my head into the crook of her neck just as I did when I was a boy. She's so light. She practically weighs nothing as I pull her into me and kiss her cheek. I inhale deeply, trying to burn the memory of her smell—the essence of her—into my brain, because I know this is the very last time that I'll ever be able to hug my mother.

That very thought causes a sob to rip out of my chest, and I cry harder than I've ever cried in my entire life.

Sunlight bounces off the chrome fixtures of the gray casket as it's lowered into the damp earth. It's almost more than I can take—the thought of knowing that she's in there heading to her final resting place—but I force a stoic expression onto my face.

I will not break down.

Most of the people here, I don't know, so I stand silently as the preacher that the funeral home recommended reads what are supposed to be words of comfort. He talks about my mother finally being able to rest in peace and we should no longer worry about her because she's in the arms of the Almighty. I would rather her be here, where I could wrap *my* arms around her. God or whoever is up there has enough. He could've spared me one of his angels.

"This is the time we should all reflect in our lives. We're never promised tomorrow. So don't put things off. Get yourself right with the Lord before your day comes," the preacher says.

While I know he means that in a religious sense, my mind works his words into something that directly relates to me. I'm tired of living a life I no longer want.

A flash of light pulls me out of my thoughts, and I scan the ridiculous number of people here for this moment. Most are reporters who are just here for a story. They could give a damn about allowing me to grieve in peace.

I mean, I just lost my fucking mother, don't I deserve that?

The constant flash of the paparazzi surrounds me. Graveyards aren't exactly private areas, and there's no law stopping the vultures from swarming in and turning this tragedy in my life into a form of entertainment.

This is why I'm sick of the celebrity that comes with my job.

I've lost myself, and my life is no longer my own. People who've never experienced this level of privacy invasion will never understand how big of a pain in the ass this lifestyle is. Money and fame are overrated and not worth losing your soul to.

The moment the cemetery workers fire up the heavy equipment to push the dirt over Mom's casket, I know my time to stand here and grieve is done. As strong as the urge is to drop to my knees and break down yet again over my loss, I refuse to put on a show for all these people.

I shove the sunglasses up my nose with my index finger and turn toward the awaiting car the funeral home provided for me. As I near the car, a tall, blond reporter rushes me with a microphone in her hand, firing questions.

"Ace, I'm Linda Bronson with *Celebrity Pop Buzz Nightly*. Will you be returning to the tour with your band, Wicked White?"

Her camera crew follows close on our heels, and I remain silent as she shoves the microphone in my face. I don't see why people give a damn about my personal life. I'm a musician. That's the only thing about me they should be worried about, but I know that making music for a living thrusts me into this crazy spotlight.

"Why did you give your band the middle finger?"

I still refuse to answer as I make it to the car and the driver opens the door so I can slide in. Once I'm inside the car, the flashes continue while they try to snag photos of me through the tinted glass.

I need to get away from all this madness. I can't take one more goddamn minute of the reporters, the dicks in the band, or Jane Ann. I'm through with it all. I never want to go back.

When the car pulls away, I shove my hair away from my face and a thought occurs to me. If I'm going to go into hiding from the world, I'm going to have to change everything about me that the world knows.

My hair.

My beard.

Hell, even my name. My stage name will have to go. No one knows the name Ace Johnson, and that's the way I intend to keep it.

The car pulls up to the hotel, and the reporters nearly break their necks as they rush me yet again as I make my way outside.

These people are fucking relentless.

After I get to my room, I pick up the phone and request the concierge to bring me a pair of scissors. I've always cut my own hair. It's a curse/blessing of growing up poor. I never had a lot of money, so cutting my own hair was something I learned to do out of necessity.

Finally, after what feels like ten minutes, the bellhop arrives with what I've requested. I go straight to work combing out my shoulder-length hair and then chopping it off with the scissors. The locks float down into the sink in front of me. Each piece flutters almost as if it's waving good-bye. Soon my hair is cropped into a short mess on the top of my head. I take care, styling it into a trendy disarray—a look that I know will throw people off my scent, making me unrecognizable. Next is my beard. It has to go too, so I take the scissors and cut away its nearly two-inch length, making it easier for the razor to shave my face smooth.

When I'm done, I stare at myself in the mirror. My nose is prominent, but not so big that it's disproportionate, and it's slightly crooked where I broke it when I fell out of a tree. It's been so long since I saw this clean-shaven guy in the mirror. For once, I finally look twenty-six years old, not ten years older because no one can see my face beneath the beard and cloak of long hair. The light brown of my eyes matches the odd color of my bronze hair. Even I have a hard time recognizing myself, so I have faith that I'll be able to slip out of here without being noticed as long as I keep my head down.

I pull on a black T-shirt and my favorite faded jeans before slipping on my boots. I don't have much in the green duffel bag I brought with me, but it has enough clothes to last me awhile. The credit cards in my wallet access all the money I have in my bank, but I know if I want to disappear without being traced, I won't be able to continuously use them. I need to pull some cash out and make do until I can find a job and get some money coming in.

When I get everything together, I take a deep breath and leave the room, setting out on a new adventure.

First things first: I need to find some transportation and an obscure place to stay. I'm ready to walk away from it all. I'll admit I feel a little lost on what I'll do with myself, but I haven't felt this free in a long time. I'm going to make Mom proud of me and be a man who stands on his own two feet and lives by his own rules.

I don't want to go back to that life. The fame—reporters always in my face—I'm done with it all. I want a life of simplicity, and that's what I'm going to set out to find.

CELEBRITY POP BUZZ NIGHTLY

The camera zooms in on Linda Bronson, the leading gossip queen on the hit television show *Celebrity Pop Buzz Nightly*. Her long, blond hair flows over her shoulders in soft waves as her blue eyes stare straight into the lens.

"Ace White, the face of the hottest up-and-coming band, Wicked White, seems to have the world at his feet. His band has just scored their fifth number-one single on the pop charts and is on track to being one of the biggest draws for concerts this year.

"Still, even with all of that, Ace White shocked the world when he gave his band the middle finger at the beginning of his sold-out show and walked off stage. No one has seen him since he disappeared from his hotel room following the funeral of the woman who raised him. He left no word with anyone who knew him. Not even his tour manager, Jane Ann Rogers, has heard from him, which has put everyone who works for Wicked White on edge. It's a mystery as to why would he walk away from everything—one I'm determined to get to the bottom of and will be making it my personal mission to uncover. For *Celebrity Pop Buzz Nightly*, I'm Linda Bronson."

Chapter 4

IRIS

She's dead.

No matter how many times those words roll through my brain, I still have a hard time believing it's true. Gran has only been gone a little over a week now, but accepting that I'll never see her walk through her front door again still cuts like a knife.

"Did you find it yet?" Birdie asks as she sits next to me on the living room floor of the trailer I grew up in while Gran raised me.

I shake my head as I continue to sift through the box of papers in front of me. "We'll never find the deed to this place at this rate."

Birdie shoves her blond hair out of her face as she continues to dig through the box in front of her. "No shit. Obviously Gee-Gee didn't believe in a filing system. Are you sure it can't be anywhere else?"

"No," I reply. "All of Gran's paperwork is in these two boxes. It has to be in here somewhere."

I flip through a couple more papers, and then bingo! "Found it!"

"Thank God," Birdie says as she shoves the box away and relief floods her dark brown eyes. "I was beginning to think it was a lost cause."

I take the paper out and examine the deed closely. Willow Acres has been in my family for generations. It all started when my great-great-grandfather opened up part of his farm for his daughter and her husband to pull a trailer onto the property to live. Since then the trailer park has expanded to now hold fifteen trailers, with most of the tenants living here since I was a kid. My place isn't glorious; it's no mansion by any means, but this one-thousand-square-foot trailer has been home to me since my mother ran off when I was four and never came back.

"Good, now we can take it down to Mr. Stern so he can get everything switched over to your name, and we can grab lunch while we're out."

I sigh as I think about the near-negative balance in my checking account. It hasn't been exactly easy since I returned here. I left almost two years ago to move to New York because I'd convinced myself that once I got there I'd be a big star on Broadway someday, but as of last week I was still just a server at a small restaurant in Brooklyn. Paying for my one-way ticket back home nearly broke the bank. If I stay here much longer, I'm going to need a job.

When Birdie takes in my silence, she wraps her slender arm around my shoulders. "Come on, Iris. It'll be my treat. I know you're starving. We've been digging through this junk all day."

Almost as if on cue my stomach rumbles loud enough for Birdie to hear, and she raises her eyebrows at me to say *told ya* before she smacks my leg. "All right. Off your ass. We're eating."

I laugh at my best friend as she snaps to her feet and then pulls me up. Birdie and I go back, way back. We had that whole sandbox love thing going on. Her grandmother, Adele, lives next door to our place, which meant Birdie was my number-one playmate when she came here every weekend while her mom partied hard. As we grew up we stayed close, because after a while, her mother left her with her grandmother too. We understood each other.

I shove my hair away from my face as I straighten my black T-shirt.

"Girl, I love those cutoff shorts. Where did you get them?" Birdie asks.

"Oh." I stare down at my too-short shorts, feeling embarrassed to be wearing something so skimpy, but they were the last clean bottoms I brought with me. "I made them. I cut off an old pair of jeans I found at a thrift store to make them."

"Creative." She fishes her keys from her purse. "Do you think we should stop at the library and see if you've gotten any responses for the ad we put on the Internet for the empty trailer?"

I nod as I follow her out the front door, locking it behind us. "Yeah. I could definitely use the rent money. Hopefully, someone responds."

"It sucks that we don't get any Internet out here," Birdie says as she unlocks her Corolla and hops inside.

Once inside with her, I buckle my seat belt. "I know. I miss having the modern conveniences of the city. My cell service doesn't even pick up the Internet out here. We're so behind in the times."

The car's engine cranks alive and Birdie backs up and starts toward the road. "As soon as you get the deed swapped over into your name for the park and are ready to go back to New York, I want to go with you."

"Really?" I can't contain the excitement in my voice. "When did you decide this?"

She shrugs. "After hearing you talk about the city all week long

25

and how much I'm missing out on by sticking around this little town. So, when you go back and get settled, let me know and I'll hop a plane."

I frown. "I never meant that it's not nice here—it is—I just don't want this life, you know? I want to see my name on a grand marquee for doing something I love, not be stuck in the trailer park for the rest of my life."

"And you will," she assures me. "It'll just be even better that I'll be there with you to see it all happen."

Willow Acres sits just outside the small village of Sarahsville, Ohio. The largest city around is Cambridge, and even that is a solid thirty-minute drive for us. We don't have much here. Most stores are mom-and-pop-type places that are privately owned. It really is like stepping back in time.

Which is exactly why I had to get out of here.

Birdie pulls up along the curb to the only attorney in town, Mr. Stern, who Gran went to for all her legal needs. I grab the deed and open the door. "It shouldn't take long. I'm just dropping this off."

Mr. Stern's office was once a private home. An old blue two story with a rickety, white picket fence and a small sign hanging from a wooden stake: William Stern, Attorney at Law.

I make my way up the sidewalk and into his office, where his plump secretary greets me with a kind smile as soon as I push open the front door. "Hi, Iris. It's so good to see you. William told me you were in town to handle Gee-Gee's estate."

I simply nod, hating the way that everyone's life seems to have gone on around me while the pain of losing Gran is still very fresh to me. "Is Mr. Stern in, Melody? I have the deed for him."

Melody's light brown braid hangs around her shoulder while her bangs are teased so high it's like she's stuck in the eighties. Like most people in this town, I've known Melody my entire life. She was the PTA president when I was in elementary school and is always into everyone's business.

She stands and takes the deed when I hand it to her, laying it on her desk before firing more questions at me. "So what was New York like? Gee-Gee said you were doing big things up there. I'd sure like to visit that place sometime, but it'll probably never happen. Big cities scare me."

"It's not that bad once you learn your way around," I say as the horn honks outside. "I'm sorry, Melody, I've got to jet. I'll catch up with you later."

"All right," she says as I wave and push my way out the front door.

I hop back in the car and Birdie's grinning at me like an idiot. "You can say thank you anytime."

"For what?" I ask with a chuckle in my voice. "I'm supposed to thank you for your impatience?"

She shakes her head. "No, for me saving your ass from Melody Schaffer. You know she would've talked you to death if I didn't save you. She's been chomping at the bit to corner you so she could invite herself to New York for a visit. This town loves to gossip. No one's ever took off to the big city like you before, so you win the prize for being most talked about around here. She would've kept digging at you until she got some kind of dirt she could break her neck telling anyone that would listen."

The thought of having Melody and her family of five in my tiny one-room apartment in Brooklyn is enough to make me shudder. And Birdie is right. Melody is the one person in this town you don't want knowing any of your business. "Thank you."

Birdie grins and slides a pair of sunglasses on her face. "Welcome. Now where to eat?"

After we get our fill at the local diner, we drive to the closest library, which is in Caldwell, the next town over, and sit down at an empty computer terminal and check the listing we posted earlier in the week for the vacant trailer. To my surprise there are a few replies in my e-mail. Two are people who obviously aren't really interested, as they respond to the ad by asking me for pictures of myself. Gross. Another I attempt to reply to, but the message fails every time, while the last only leaves a phone number and nothing more.

After a long moment of debate on what to do with the number, I sigh and close out the web page.

"What are you doing?" Birdie asks. "Don't you think you should call that number?"

"No," I answer immediately. "Who replies with only a phone number? That's weird and creepy as hell."

She shrugs. "Yeah, but it could mean money."

I furrow my brow at her. "Do you really want to take a chance and let some crazy serial killer move in next to me and your grandmother?"

She rolls her eyes. "I highly doubt that's going to happen. Besides, whoever this person is can't be any crazier than Jeremy. That guy is completely off his hinges."

Jeremy is the newest tenant at Willow. He moved into one of Gran's rentals right before she had her first heart attack six months ago, and she didn't have the strength to deal with kicking him out when all the people around him complained. He's rude and a constant nuisance to all the other tenants with his loud-ass cars and parties. He's one of the things on my checklist to deal with while I'm here getting things settled.

My shoulders sag, and I wish I wasn't this desperate for money, but the truth is I'm completely broke. Not only did Mr. Stern inform me at the will reading that I get everything that my gran owned, I get to incur her debt too. Apparently, she'd forgotten to pay property taxes on Willow Acres for quite some time, and the state is looking to collect its money. If I can't come up with the money, the state will come and take the property, and I'm not sure where that leaves everyone who lives there. I can't allow them to be thrown out of their homes.

The only way I have a shot in hell at saving the place is to make sure that every single trailer is inhabited. So, like it or not, this crazy number is my only real lead to finding an interested, paying tenant.

I open the web browser and reopen the e-mail so I can jot the number down. "You're right, Birdie. Something is better than nothing at this point."

She wraps her arm around my shoulders. "Don't worry, Iris. We'll find someone soon."

It's crazy, but all my hope now rests on this one strange number.

ACE

After blowing up a map of Ohio on my phone, the small town of Sarahsville catches my eye. It's almost like fate calling to me, since my mother's name was Sarah. What better place to hide in? It'll almost be like she's protecting me.

I make one last major purchase with my black American Express, a black Harley-Davidson Sportster, because it's better than hitchhiking. I also pick up a guitar from a local pawn shop and withdraw five thousand dollars from the bank. Hopefully Columbus will be the last place they can trace my whereabouts to before I disappear. Walmart is last on my list to hit before I take off. I purchase a prepaid cell with cash and then look online to find a place to rent. I find only one, and it seems like it's probably a dump, which makes it perfect. No one would ever expect me to be living in some broken-down trailer park in the middle of nowhere.

I quickly fire a reply to the ad and leave only my phone number before I set off on the hour-and-a-half trip to my new little city.

The ride is cold, and maybe I should've rethought my plan on using a motorcycle as my form of transportation, considering it's October in Ohio. The temperature here can fluctuate all over the place this time of the year. It's been a long time since I've lived here, and I want to kick myself for not remembering this isn't the California weather that I'm used to.

I turn off the main interstate and head down a county highway for the last thirty minutes of my drive and then coast into the small town of Sarahsville, reading the sign alerting me to the fact there's a population of only 168 people. I may have found a more anonymous place than expected.

I pull into a local grocery and park my bike. The Oakley sunglasses covering my eyes darken my vision as I step inside, so I push them up on top of my head. A cowbell hanging over the door rings to announce my presence.

"Hello?" I call, a little uneasy being alone in here.

"Be with you in a minute," an older man's voice calls from a little room behind the counter.

A moment later, a gray-headed man pokes his head out of the room. "Can I help you, son?"

I clear my throat. "I'm looking for Willow Acres. Can you tell me where to find it?"

"Willow Acres, you say?" He steps out of the room and I take in the lanky man who's probably in his sixties. His faded flannel shirt and jeans about two sizes too big tell me he's either lost a lot of weight suddenly or he doesn't have enough money to buy proper sizes. He narrows his green eyes at me, causing his bushy white eyebrows to pull inward. "You ain't from the state, are you, because if you are, you'll just have to find it on your own."

I laugh at the old man's protective tone. "No, sir. I'm just looking for a place to rent."

He scratches at his day-old beard. "Well, in that case, I'll write down the directions for you. The name's Pete."

I extend my hand to him, which he gives a hearty shake almost immediately. "Ace Johnson."

Pete grabs a scrap piece of paper from under his counter and draws me a detailed map of how to get out to the trailer park. After explaining the directions to me thoroughly, he hands me the paper. "Tell Iris that Pete sent ya. I'll warn you, Willow Acres isn't much to look at, but Iris Easton is a good girl and she'll be fair with you, so try not to judge it too harshly when you first pull up."

I give him a small smile. "Yes, sir."

I take the paper, feeling pretty confident that I can find my way, and stuff it into the back pocket of my jeans. I fire up my bike and take the roads as directed, and it takes me only about five minutes to make it the entrance of Willow Acres as labeled by an old, faded green sign with white lettering.

The trailers in the park are much older than I expected—most appearing like something built back in the seventies and not much upkeep done on them since then. It's clean around the place, no garbage or anything lying around, but everything just looks so worn down. Windows are taped shut with duct tape to fix broken glass panes on a couple of the places, and it makes me think twice about wanting to stay here. It makes me think some seedy characters live here, and I have no desire to live in a crack den.

I wanted to hide, but this place may be too obscure and backwoods even for me.

I make it to the second trailer in the lot. It's all white with a little plot of flowers surrounding the small patch of Astroturf that's laid out over the concrete in front of the place. A green-and-white sign matching the one out front hangs by the door and reads Office. I park my bike out front and walk up the small wooden porch steps and knock on the front door.

"Just a minute!" A woman calls as I hear some rustling inside.

The lock on the door clicks and the door opens, revealing one of the most breathtaking women I've ever seen. Her long, dark hair falls over her shoulders in soft waves; her makeup is light, revealing her naturally smooth complexion, which causes her green eyes to sparkle. Her V-cut T-shirt and tight-fitting jeans hug her body's hourglass curves like a glove.

I stand there completely tongue-tied, checking her out from head to toe. It's not until I take in the expression on her face that I start to worry. Her full pink lips gape open in an *O* shape as she stares at my face. I pause, suddenly afraid that this place might not be as far out in the sticks as I hoped if she does recognize me.

Instantly, I'm attracted to this woman and I become angry with myself for feeling this way. Now is not the time to be thinking about a woman. I don't plan on sticking in one place too long, and I'll be damned if I allow some beauty to get into my head and make me change my plans. If she gets too close and I get too comfortable, I'll reveal all my secrets to her, and I can't let that happen.

The best thing I can do is be a complete dick to her and keep things between us strictly business.

She shakes her head as if pulling herself out of a daze before she licks her lips. "Can I help you?"

I pull the sunglasses from my eyes in order to make eye contact with her. "I'm here to see Iris about the trailer for rent? I e-mailed earlier with my number, but I figured I'd take a chance and stop by to see if it was still available?"

"You?" she questions. "You want to move into one of *my* rentals? *Here?*"

"Yeah? What of it?" I fire back.

She does a double take of my clothing and then glances out to my bike parked outside of her place. "You just don't seem like the type."

I shake my head. "Don't pretend like you know me or *my type*. Look, I don't have all day. Do you have the place or not?"

She flinches at my tone. "I do, but you don't have to be a complete asshole to me."

Her eyes narrow, and for a moment I think she's about to tell me to hit the road for my rudeness, but she doesn't. Instead, she sighs and shakes her head before reaching to the left of the door, grabbing a set of keys that must've been hanging on the wall. "Come on. I'll show you to the trailer."

I follow behind her to the blue-and-white trailer next to the office, the very first on the lot. Even though I shouldn't, I allow my eyes to fixate on the sway of her little round ass in those jeans as she walks in front of me. It's like the devil put a temptation in the form of this sexy little vixen before me to force me to give up and go running back to the label and beg their forgiveness.

When she turns around, I jerk my gaze away from her and focus anywhere but on her. I want to appear absolutely put off by her, so she'll hate me and stay as far away from me as possible.

Iris makes her way up the two little wooden steps and unlocks the rickety front door with its tiny triangle window. She shoves open the door and steps inside, and I go in after.

The first thing that hits me is the musty odor, like it hasn't been lived in for years and the last tenant was a seventy-year-old crazy cat lady. The next thing is the stained burgundy carpet and clashing flamingo-pink furniture and decor. Like the outside, it's clean in here, just very old and outdated.

"Sorry about the smell," Iris says as she stands back, allowing me to take a look around. "It's been closed up in here for quite a while, but everything is clean. The hot water works fine and there's no issues with the electrical that I'm aware of. It comes fully furnished."

I walk around the room. The kitchen and living room are practically the same space, and in the ad the place was listed as a two bedroom, which is more than enough space for me. "How much is it again?"

"It's a four-hundred-dollar deposit plus another four hundred for the first month's rent, so eight hundred in total to move in."

Before she has a chance to say another word, I say, "I'll take it."

She lifts her eyebrows in surprise. "You will? Okay . . . well . . . let's see . . . I need you to come back to the office and fill out a renter's agreement. Rent will be due on the first of every month, and there's a twenty-five-dollar late charge if you're more than a week late."

"Fair enough."

Her green eyes focus on my face as if she's attempting to figure me out, and she holds out the keys to me. "Welcome to the neighborhood, Mister . . ."

"Johnson, Ace Johnson." I tell her my real name, not the one I'm known to the world by, but don't offer a smile.

I have to resist her allure no matter how nice she is to me.

When I don't go into any more details about myself, she says, "Come on. Let's get that paperwork done."

As soon as I fill out the form, I give Iris eight hundred dollars in cash and walk out of the office. I can tell she believes I'm an asshole, and I hate that things have to be that way, because she seems nice, but it's best for both of us if we don't get involved. The crazy life I lead would chew up and spit out a nice little country bumpkin like Iris.

Once I leave, I grab my bike and push it over to the designated parking area next to my trailer, go inside, and shut myself off from the world.

Chapter 6

IRIS

I pull back the curtain just enough so that I can stare outside at my astonishingly sexy new neighbor as he washes his motorcycle. His bronze hair reflects a lot of the subtle undertones that snake through it as he stands in the sunlight with his red flannel shirt rolled up to his elbows. His dark-washed jeans hug his tight backside while he inspects every inch of the machine in front of him, and it causes me to bite my lip. It's been a week since he moved in, and I still don't know a single thing about him other than the fact he's absurdly handsome and kind of an asshole. I can't figure him out—why a guy like him is not only single but such a recluse.

"He's going to catch you stalking him," Birdie says as she pours a cup of coffee.

Immediately, I let the white curtain fall back into place and fire back, "I'm not stalking him."

She raises one eyebrow at me and smirks as she fills another cup. "Um, have you forgotten who you're talking to here? I can always tell when you're lying. Your nose twitch gives you away every time."

I stop midtwitch and huff as I walk over and pick up the cup she's set out for me and throw a scoop of sugar in with a dash of French vanilla creamer. "I'm not stalking him, *exactly*. It's more like a nagging curiosity about him that just won't go away. He's not from around here, and I can't figure out why a guy that looks like him would ever want to move into that run-down place next door."

Birdie shakes her head as she leans against the counter. "You saying this place isn't good enough for him? It's good enough for us, why not him?"

I swallow a sip of the piping-hot liquid from my cup. "Did you see the bike he rode in on? And how about those clothes? I've seen flannel shirts and detailed stitched jeans like the ones he wears—they aren't cheap. It seems like he can afford more than a four-hundred-dollar-a-month trailer in the middle of nowhere."

She sighs. "You don't know him, Iris. He could be a total creeper running from the law or something. Just because he's hot doesn't mean he doesn't have a fucked-up past. If you're smart, you'd give him the privacy he's obviously after. Getting mixed up with a guy like him is bad news."

"You're probably right, but I can't help being curious," I admit.

Birdie stares at me over her coffee cup. "That curiosity might lead you to trouble. You need to nip that shit in the butt."

I laugh. "You mean bud."

She waves me off dismissively. "Bud—butt. You know what I meant."

A short time later, Birdie heads out for work. When I walk her to the door, I notice my reclusive next-door neighbor still outside, waxing his bike. I lean against the door frame and wave good-bye as my best friend hops in her car and pulls away while honking the horn.

The commotion catches Ace's attention and he glances back to where I'm standing. When his gaze locks with mine, my breath actually catches, and I wonder if he and I should start over since we aren't exactly on neighborly terms.

I lift my hand in greeting, but quickly jerk it down when his expression turns into a blatant scowl pointed in my direction.

I huff, completely put off by his utter rudeness, and slam the door.

What's his freaking problem?

I've never in my life had someone be such an ass to me.

The angry roar of his motorcycle coming to life rumbles the thin walls of my trailer as he mashes the gas and heads down the road.

Maybe Birdie is right. Ace Johnson could very well be hiding something, and I think it's my duty as the new owner of Willow Acres to find out just what that could be, whether he likes me or not. Looks like I'm going to have to kill him with kindness. That's the way Gran always taught me to treat people who were mean to me. Let's hope it works on Ace.

All afternoon I wait on Ace's return so I can march over and fire some questions off at him, but as the time passes I find myself absolutely out of my mind with boredom with no Internet or cable service here. New York has certainly spoiled me with its conveniences.

As I sit on the small wooden porch outside my front door, I notice how unruly the grass has become around the property. Our lawn service quit two weeks ago when I explained that I didn't have enough money to pay them. They didn't trust that I would be good for it after the first of the month when all of the rents start coming in. It didn't matter to them that Gran had just passed away and that

I'm still struggling to figure things out, all that mattered to them was that they get paid, which I understand. It just sucks for me, making this overgrown lawn one more thing I have to deal with.

I push myself up and walk through the yard, the grass tickling my ankles from its height as I make my way to the shed at the back of the trailer. Inside I find an old push mower that Gran bought when I was just a kid. She quit using it herself a few years back when she hit her midfifties, saying she was too old to push the damn thing around and upping the lot rent to hire the lawn service.

I drag the mower out onto the grass and try to remember exactly how to start this thing. I clutch the lever attached to the handle and grab the pulley and yank with all my might, yet nothing happens. I know this is how to start it. I used to mow all this grass as a teenager, helping Gran out around the place, so I'm not sure what the problem is here. After doing the same thing over and over about ten times, I shove my hands on my hips and curse at the stupid machine, fighting back the urge to kick it.

The sound of an approaching motorcycle causes me to roll my eyes.

Great. He would come back just when I decide to find something to keep me busy, getting grease and dirt all over my hands in the process. My interrogation of him will have to wait until some other time now.

I do my best to ignore the fact that Ace has returned and refocus on starting the lawn mower. I yank one more time, and when nothing happens, I curse loudly, out of pure frustration, "Fucking piece of shit!"

"Problems?"

I turn to see Ace standing before me with his arms crossed over his broad chest, looking more godlike than ever, staring at me expectantly with those brown eyes of his.

My shoulders sag, as I hate admitting defeat to this man. He's such a crass know-it-all. "I can't get it to start."

He nods but doesn't say anything else as he walks over beside me. The smell of soap and spice fills my nose, and I'm tempted to lean in closer to him and take a long whiff. His scent makes me want to lick him, but I fight hard to restrain myself, because that wouldn't go over well.

The thick cords in his arms move after he stoops down and turns a small silver cap on the engine of the machine. "Did you check the gas?"

My cheeks redden as embarrassment floods through me. "I forgot about that."

He closes one eye and peers down into the hole before shaking his head. "It's bone dry." He stares up at me. "How long have you owned this place?"

"I just inherited from my gran two weeks ago when she passed. Truthfully, I'm a little lost at how I'm supposed to keep the place running. I don't know how she managed it all these years."

It's almost as if something resonates with him, because his normal scowl is replaced with a frown. "I'm sorry to hear about your gran. Were you all close?"

I nod. "She raised me and was the closest thing to a mom I ever had."

Ace sighs as he rubs the back of his neck. "I'll tell you what. If you knock fifty bucks a month off the rent, I'll do all the lawn work around here. That'll make one less burden you have to worry about."

"Deal!" I say a little too enthusiastically, and Ace's eyebrows draw in like he's aggravated by my excitement, but I go ahead and attempt to start our relationship over. "I really think we got started off on the wrong foot."

Ace holds up a hand, cutting me off. "This in no way means we're friends. I'm just looking for ways to save myself some money. Got it?"

I flinch as the short tone he takes with me returns, and it pisses me off that he feels like he has the right to treat me like this. Maybe Gran's idea to be nice isn't meant for this situation, because he obviously has no interest in making amends. "Whatever."

I turn and walk inside the trailer to finish going through some of Gran's things to distract myself from the beautiful asshole who lives next door.

When Ace returns from the gas station, the constant sound of the mower working at chopping down the grass echoes through Willow Acres. At least the tidiness around the park that Gran prided herself on so much is getting back to normal. "We might be poor, but that's no excuse to live like animals" is what Gran would always say.

I make myself some lemonade in the kitchen and then sit outside on the steps as I wait for Birdie to return home from her job as a daytime bartender at a small club in Cambridge. She's been working so hard to worm her way into her boss's good graces. Her goal of obtaining an evening shift position is pretty close to being attained. She's been at Angel's for only three months, and she's already next on the list for a shift that's known for the best tips. I'm proud of how hard she works. My friend has a great work ethic.

The loud rumble of Jeremy's beat-up 1990s-model Trans Am catches my attention just in time for me to see him come to a skidding halt in front of my place. His T-tops are open, and he doesn't even bother using his door as he hoists himself out of the car. He tucks his long, sandy-blond hair behind his ears as he approaches me. The T-shirt covering his slim body has the sleeves cut off, and the jeans he has on are filthy, like he's been rolling around in mud.

I hope he's bringing the rent he's two weeks late paying.

I give him a polite smile, hoping he's not coming to me to ask for another week to pay his rent. "Hey, Jeremy."

Jeremy takes that as an invitation and walks up to the porch where I'm sitting and props one leg up beside me on the step. His green eyes bore into me as he leers down at me in a way that makes me wish I had about fifteen layers of clothes covering my body.

"Iris, I've got your rent." He leans back and pulls a wad of cash from his back pocket and hands it to me. "My dick boss was late paying me."

The worn money slides through my fingers as I count it in front of him. When I count out only four hundred dollars, I ask, "Where's the late fee?"

He makes a sour face. "Why the fuck are you going to charge me a late fee? I told you last week that I would be late. It wasn't my fault that my boss didn't pay me until today."

If he had been nice about the situation, I probably would have let the twenty-five-dollar fee go, but because he's being a complete jackass about it, I'm pressing the issue. I set the money down on the step beside me and pick up my glass of lemonade. "I never said that you wouldn't have to pay that. You signed a contract—"

"Fuck your contract, bitch!" Jeremy knocks the glass of lemonade out of my hand, causing me to gasp and flinch because I'm not sure if he's going to swing at my face next. The liquid spills as the glass crashes down on the concrete and shatters into a hundred pieces. "You got your money. Be grateful for that."

"That's enough!" Ace's deep voice cuts between me and Jeremy.

Jeremy's back tenses and he straightens and twists his head from side to side like he's readying himself for a fight. He pushes himself away from the step and turns to face Ace, who is standing a few feet away. "I think you need to mind your own business, pretty boy. You don't want me to mess up that face of yours, so go back to wherever you fucking came from. This here, it's between me and Iris."

Ace balls his fists at his sides. "I'm only going to tell you one time, back the fuck away from her."

Jeremy laughs as he grabs a knife from his pocket and flips it open. "Or you'll what?" Ace takes a step back and raises his hands, causing Jeremy to smirk. "That's what I thought, tough guy. If you know what's good for ya, you'll get the hell out of here."

Ace narrows his eyes at Jeremy. "I'm not leaving her with you."

My heart leaps into my throat as Jeremy begins circling Ace with his drawn knife. Fear paralyzes me, as I struggle to sort through my brain for what's the right thing to do in this situation. Do I jump between them, risking my own life, or let Ace handle it?

I clutch my chest as the realization hits that I have to do something. This guy barely knows me. I can't allow him to get hurt.

I jump up from my seat and take a hesitant step toward Jeremy before placing my hand on his arm. "That's enough. This is crazy. Stop!"

Jeremy seizes the opportunity and shoves me with his free hand so hard into the trailer behind me that the wind whooshes from my lungs.

A growl rips from Ace's throat as he hits Jeremy's arm, knocking the knife from his hand before blasting him with a fist in the face. The moment Ace's knuckles make contact with Jeremy's nose, an audible crunch sounds and blood pours down Jeremy's face.

"Oh, God," Jeremy cries as he covers his face with both hands and doubles over in pain. "You broke my nose."

Ace stands there, fists drawn and chest heaving while keeping his eyes trained on Jeremy. "I'll break a lot more if you don't leave. Now."

Those words do not need to be spoken twice, as Jeremy turns tail and stumbles to his car. "This isn't over, asshole."

"Yes it is. Touch her again and I will annihilate you." Ace's menacing words are a dark warning to Jeremy—one I pray he takes seriously, because I don't want the poor guy's blood on my hands. I obviously don't know what Ace is capable of.

This time Jeremy opens the driver's door of his car, flings himself inside, and fires up the roaring engine. A thick cloud of dust wafts around as the tires of the Trans Am spin before he speeds away.

It's then I notice I'm still leaning against the trailer, frozen, in the same position I was just knocked into.

Ace turns to me once the Trans Am is out of sight, concern etched into his features. "You okay?"

I shove my hair back from my face and inspect the rest of me to confirm there's no damage. "Yes. I think so."

He gives me a curt nod and turns his back to me, not offering me a bit of explanation on why he intervened on my behalf the way he did. "Ace, wait."

Midstride, he pauses but doesn't face me. He turns his head to the side so that I can see his beautiful profile. "For what?"

I rush to him and allow my eyes to flit over his body, frantically searching for any injuries. When they finally land on his bloody knuckles, I reach down without permission and pull his hand up for inspection. "You're hurt."

As I run my fingers gently over his skin, he closes his eyes like my touch is painful. "I'm fine."

"Are you going to tell me why you did that?" I ask quietly.

"I need a reason to save a woman from being bullied from some jerkoff who was determined to hurt her?" he says as he opens his eyes to gaze upon me. His eyes serious, and expression unreadable.

"Yes, if the woman you save is obviously one you hate," I reply.

"I don't hate you." He hesitates for a beat and then shakes his head. "I just need to stay away from you."

The answer he gives me still isn't enough to satisfy my curious brain. "That makes no sense. Tell me why you feel that way."

He lets out an exasperated sigh. "Just let it go, Iris. Pushing this issue will only be dangerous for us both."

I open my mouth to argue with him once again, but he doesn't give me the opportunity before he stalks off, putting as much distance between us as he can.

ACE

The cold shocks the heated skin on my knuckles as I shove my hand into a bowl full of ice. Beating the shit out of some local redneck isn't exactly how I planned on beginning my low-key life here in Sarahsville, but there is no way I'm just going to stand by and let some douche bag talk to Iris that way and get away with it.

Not going to happen.

The fucker is lucky I didn't kill him. The thought of ending his miserable existence crossed my mind the moment he put his hands on her, and he's lucky I have enough self-control to reel myself back from going off the deep end. I've been known to go a little berserk when I'm angry, which is something I'm not proud of, because I've learned through time usually it's better to keep a cool head. Being around Jane Ann for so long tamed me quite a bit. What losing my temper would do to my career if the media ever got wind of it made me think twice before I acted out, and it ended up making me soft—a fucking pushover yes-man—but there are times when going a little crazy is needed in a situation. I would do anything to protect someone I care about.

If this incident today had happened five years ago, before Jane Ann discovered me, Jeremy would've not been able to walk away without the help of some medical assistance.

I grab a cold beer from the fridge and then thrust my throbbing hand back down into the ice. Being around this girl is not good. The overwhelming urge I have to protect her and take care of her now that I know she's all alone in this world like me is pretty damn strong. Hell, look at what already happened. I haven't gotten that out of control in a long time. But she needed the help. I have this feeling down in my gut that I'm supposed to be the one to look out for her.

I should do the right thing and hop on my bike and put as much distance between me and this place as possible. Eventually the media circus will find me, and the craziness of my world will be brought down all around Iris and her peaceful little existence, and she doesn't deserve that.

Just before dark there's a knock at my door. I push myself off the couch, bringing my beer with me as I fling the water away from my fucked-up hand and flex my sore fingers.

When I open the door, Iris stands there with a plate full of cookies wrapped in cellophane. She smiles, and this irks me because no matter how big of a dick I am to this girl, she still won't give up being friendly to me.

"What?" I say a little more briskly than I mean to, and it causes her to flinch.

She swallows hard. "I brought you a peace offering." She tilts the plate a little to draw my attention to the chocolate chip cookies. "And since you're new in town, I thought maybe you'd want to come with us tonight to a bar in Cambridge to get out of this place for a while."

"Which bar?" This invitation is tempting. So tempting, in fact, for a moment I consider saying yes. Selfishly, I crave more time with her.

She smiles, and I swear to God my heart skips a beat. "My friend Birdie and I are going to the bar she works at, Angel's. You game?"

The thought of being out somewhere with this beautiful girl before me, dancing with her, holding her body against mine, is almost worth being recognized for. But I know if I'm playing it smart, I can't be seen out with anyone. If one person notices me and is able to figure out who I am, the media and Jane Ann will be all over me before I have a chance to ditch them again. I'll be forced to go back on tour and into a life that I no longer want to lead. I'm not ready to face that yet.

I sigh and hold up my beer. "Why would I leave when I got all the booze I need right here?"

Her green eyes flick over to my beer and then back to meet my gaze. "I was hoping we could start over—at least be friendly toward one another."

It makes me more excited inside than I'm comfortable admitting that she wants me around her, but still I can't let my guard down and get too comfortable here.

I let out a heavy breath. I guess I can I turn down the dick factor just a touch; God knows she's really done nothing to deserve my cruelty. "Some other time, maybe. Be safe."

Iris's bottom lip juts out a bit as she pouts. "Okay, then. I guess

I'll see you around." She halts midturn and holds out the plate in front of her. "Hope you like them. I made them myself."

I raise my eyebrow. "They're not poisoned?"

She laughs. "No. The last thing I would ever want to do is hurt my knight in shining armor."

She doesn't say anything else, simply turns and leaves me standing there with a plate full of cookies that she made especially for me. My heart does a double thump in my chest at the thought of being her hero, but it's not good that she sees me in that light.

A kind heart like hers isn't something that's easily found. Why couldn't I have met her before I decided to take my ass into hiding and shut out the entire world? I can't allow myself to get to know this girl, because our entire relationship would be built on nothing but lies and deceit. But besides all that, fame and the media would eat a nice girl like her alive.

Close to nine, laughter from Iris and her friend spill into my trailer through the open window in my kitchen that faces Iris's place. I know I shouldn't, but I can't help myself from rushing over to the nearest window and taking a peek.

Iris's long, brown hair is down, bouncing around her bare shoulders with each step as she makes her way to Birdie's Corolla. The halter top she has on screams clubbing clothes, and paired with the jean skirt she's wearing that shows off her long, toned legs, is just the right amount of sexy.

I pull the knuckle I didn't even realize I was biting away from my teeth as she jumps in the car.

The idea of her being out there tonight, alone, drives me nuts. The mere thought of another man touching that smooth, soft skin that I long to caress with my own hands is enough to make me go out of my mind with jealousy.

As I grab the keys to my bike, I quickly convince myself that following her tonight is purely for her safety. I need to be there to protect her and watch out for her. I won't allow another man to put his hands on her like Jeremy did today. She needs me.

After driving thirty minutes to Cambridge, I stop at the first gas station I come to and ask for directions to the bar Iris said she would be at. It doesn't take me long to find Angel's and spot Birdie's little white Corolla parked outside.

It's not a big place by any means, but judging from its two-story brick exterior, it should be plenty big enough for me to move around inside without Iris noticing me watching her like a total creeper.

I park my bike around the side of the building and then make my way up to the bald-headed bouncer wearing a black T-shirt that reads "Angel's" across the chest.

"ID," he asks as I approach.

I fish my wallet from the back pocket of my jeans before handing him my driver's license. Momentary panic sets in as the tank of a man scrutinizes my identification card a little longer than necessary before handing it back to me. "Have a good time."

Whew. That was close. For a moment there I thought the haircut and shave wouldn't be enough to throw a true fan off my scent, but lucky for me, the guy didn't let on that he knew who I was even if he did. He's probably not exactly a pop music fan.

I stuff my wallet back into my pocket and then dip inside. The lights are dimmed low, but the sunken dance floor is lit up with a rainbow of swirling lights that keep time to the beat of the song the DJ's playing.

The crowd parts on the dance floor and I spot Iris immediately. Her long hair falls in soft waves as she sways her hips to the beat and sings along to the country song that's being spun. I don't know the song at all because I don't listen to that genre of music, but I find myself mesmerized by the hypnotic rhythm as I train my gaze on Iris. Her fucking smile could light up this entire goddamn room.

"Sugar, can I get you a beer?" I turn to the bottle-blond twentysomething waitress who's balancing a tray against her hip while snapping her gum as she waits on my response.

I nod. "Yeah, Bud Light in a bottle."

"You got it," she answers before she scampers off just as quickly as she appeared.

I lean against a nearby column as I continue to watch Iris. She doesn't know it yet, but it's so unlucky for her that I'm this interested. Eventually my old life will catch up to me. Jane Ann won't stop looking for me as long as I'm costing her money, and Iris will be caught in the media crossfire if they find me here hiding with her, and that makes me feel guilty.

It's cruel of me to be so selfish, but I can't seem to stop myself from wanting to be near her. I can't explain it, but I can't help but be drawn to her. Besides the fact that she's fucking beautiful, she's been nothing but kind to me since I arrived, even though I've been a complete jackass to her, which makes me want her even more. It's like she can put up with my moody ass and still see through to the inner part of me that's good.

Hell, maybe I'm drawn to her so much because I've been around such shit people lately that I need something positive in my life. Either way, though, I need to fight the urge to claim her as my own, because she never asked for my crazy life to be brought on her.

A group of guys who seem to be in their midtwenties saunter over to the edge of the dance floor. Most of them seem harmless, cracking jokes and laughing together, just out to have a good time while checking out the girls on the floor, but one catches my eye, making my hair stand up on end.

There's nothing special about the guy, really. He's of average height and build, with a baseball cap turned backward covering his shaggy brown hair, but what makes me notice him is how he hasn't been able to tear his eyes away from Iris. It's hard to miss Iris because she's simply breathtaking, and I understand any man would be fucking blind if he didn't notice her, but he's fixated on her, studying her, like he's planning to make a move. I don't fucking like it.

Unable to stop myself, I ball my fists up at the thought of this douche bag getting to touch her. I don't think I'll be able to stop myself from yanking him off her, which is crazy because she might be into the guy. It's not my place to interfere, only to keep her safe if she needs me.

"Here you go, sugar." The waitress pulls me out of my anger-filled daze as she hands me the beer.

I lay a ten-dollar bill on her tray. "Keep the change."

The blond doesn't immediately go away. Instead, she stands there, biting her lip. "I'm not usually so forward, but I get off in a couple of hours and thought maybe since you're here alone, you're looking for a good time. I wouldn't mind being your just-for-tonight girl."

I take a long pull from my beer as I debate her offer. Maybe if I take this girl back to her place and screw her brains out, this twisted mess of feelings I'm experiencing over Iris will go away.

But the crazy thing is, the thought of being with this random girl repulses me. I've had her type many times in the form of my groupies. The sex is meaningless. Those women were just out to use me. None of them ever really cared about me. They cared about my celebrity and the bragging rights being with me gave them, and I'm not in the mood to deal with that kind of bullshit right now. Besides, my brain is fixated on Iris, and I'd rather have no one if I can't have her.

"I don't think so, doll," I tell her, causing the flirtatious smile to drop from her face and an angry scowl to replace it.

"Your loss, asshole," she snarls before she turns and walks away.

The short interaction I had with the waitress caused me to take my sights off Iris, but I quickly find her again, only this time she's not dancing alone.

The same fucker who was stalking her moments ago now has his hands gripping her shoulders as he grinds his crotch into her ass. I try to remain calm and not rush out there like a crazed psycho as I watch the scene in front of me unfold.

At first, it appears that Iris might be having fun as she rolls her eyes at Birdie, who's dancing in front of her, but then when Iris steps away from the man to distance herself, he refuses to give up, shoving himself right back into her backside.

I stiffen and take a step forward but halt the moment Iris turns and shoves the man away from her. That same spunk she shows me when I'm being a rude jackass is amplified tenfold as she yells at the man to back off.

I didn't know she could handle herself like that. Maybe I should've given her a little more credit for being able to put Jeremy in his place before I jumped in the middle of the situation to defend her. But I'm quickly learning when it comes to her I can't seem to help myself from defending her.

When the man tries to touch her again, Iris scowls at him before grabbing Birdie by the arm and dragging her to the other side of the dance floor. The guy watches for a long moment like he's debating following Iris, trying to dance with her yet again, but ultimately decides against it as he rejoins his friends at the edge of the floor.

There's only four of them, and I'm angry enough that I might have a shot at getting a few good punches in before his buddies tear me off him. The prick needs to be taught a fucking lesson in manners. Ultimately, I decide to bide my time until I can get him alone, wanting to keep things private. A roomful of witnesses won't be ideal.

The rest of the night Iris keeps jumping up to the bar and taking shot after shot in between songs while I notice Birdie restrains herself, probably seeing as how she has to drive back home. The two women never notice me in the bar. Turns out I'm pretty good at hiding if I don't want to be found, but I keep my watchful eyes trained on Iris and the guy who got a little rough with her earlier.

I'm not a fan of touching anyone without permission. It's an invasion of privacy—one I know about all too well. Guys like this douche bag from the bar are the type of people who decide if they want something from somebody, they'll just take it. I lived in a couple foster homes where the people that were supposed to be my protectors felt they had the right to lay their hands on me, some even sexually. It wasn't until I got placed with Sarah that I felt safe and learned not everyone did that. That's why I vowed to myself that I'd always protect vulnerable people when I could.

Still stewing, I keep my eye on the group of guys, allowing my protective jealousy to cloud my mind, which makes it impossible for me to forget how he pawed her earlier.

When he detaches himself from the group, I double-check that Iris and Birdie are now sitting safely at a corner booth before I follow him into the men's room.

He stumbles as he makes his way over to the urinal and I lock us inside the restroom. Alone. I pull the hood of my sweatshirt over my head and begin to stalk my unsuspecting prey.

Without warning, I rush over and grab the back of his head and slam his forehead into the wall. A loud thud echoes around the tiny room and his hat falls to the floor by our feet.

"Ah, oh," the drunken man cries as he covers his face with his hands, but he doesn't look directly at me, merely squeezes his eyes shut as he's riddled with pain.

I grab a fistful of his hair and yank his head back so I can whisper in his ear, "You should think twice about putting your hands on a woman without a fucking invitation. The next guy you run into might not be as nice as me."

I shove his head forward and he stumbles a bit as I turn and rush out of the small, urine-smelling room.

IRIS

I raise the "purple hooter" shot to Birdie as the tingle of all the alcohol I've consumed tonight washes through my entire body. "To the bestest friend a girl could ever ask for. Birdie, I love ya!"

"Oh, God. Now I know you're toasted." Birdie laughs and rolls her brown eyes.

I close one eye to bring her better into focus. "How?"

She grins. "When you start telling me that you love me, I know you're at your limit. You're such a happy drunk."

I press the glass to my lips and throw my head back as I drink the contents of the glass down in one shot and then giggle, clapping my hands. "One more."

Birdie shakes her head. "No way! I'm not carrying your drunk ass home tonight."

I stick my tongue out at her. "Party pooper."

She pushes her way out of the booth we're sitting in. "One more dance, and then let's hit the road. I've got to come back here tomorrow to work."

We make our way out on the floor and grind together as we laugh and sing along to the music. The only semidecent-looking guy to come on to me tonight was a total creeper and disappeared after I shoved him away when he got a little handsy while whispering he was going to fuck me raw behind the building. I'm no slut and I don't appreciate being treated like one.

Birdie glances around the bar. "There are absolutely no cute guys here."

I turn to take in the faces around me to confirm Birdie's complaint when my eyes land on a pair of warm brown eyes trained on every move I make.

Ace leans casually against a large black column as he sips a beer while openly watching me. I don't know how I missed him before. The black hooded sweatshirt he's wearing must've hidden him in the shadows of the club. His hair is styled in the same disarray of sexiness that he typically rocks while those damn sexy blue jeans hang low on his hips. I swear the man gets sexier every time I see him.

Birdie stops dancing and follows my line of sight before gasping. "How long has he been here?"

I bite my bottom lip, finding it extremely difficult to tear my eyes away from his intense stare. "I'm not sure. I just spotted him."

She grabs my arm and leans toward me, yelling over the music, "I thought you said he wasn't coming?"

I shrug. "That's what he told me."

"Looks like he changed his mind," she says.

"It appears so."

Instinctively, my body pulls itself in his direction. It's so superficial to say this, but the first thing I always notice about Ace is how insanely beautiful he is. The next thing is his intensity. He's always so focused and serious, and it's very alluring. I want to know his secret. I want to know what he's hiding, and why he's so hot and cold with me.

"Iris? Where are you going?" Birdie asks as I take a step toward him. "Don't you think it's a bit stalkerish for him to come here and not approach you, but just stare at you like that?"

I pull away from her grasp and laugh as I try to reassure her. "I invited him. I'm glad he's here."

Bodies swaying to the beat block my path, and I push, pull, and squeeze until I make it off the floor with Birdie close on my heels. My eyes dart back to the spot where I last spotted Ace, but he's nowhere to be seen.

I stand there, completely frazzled as I shove my hair back and search the sea of faces one by one, hoping he's merely just moved. A long sigh pours out of me as Birdie finds her spot next to me.

"Where did he go?" Birdie asks as she begins looking around too.

"No clue," I answer and am glad for the loud country music covering the pouting tone in my voice. "I don't know why he would come here and then run away when he knows I'm about to approach him."

"You should stay away from that guy, Iris. He seems like nothing but a bunch of trouble to me—sexy trouble, but trouble nonetheless."

She's right, but that doesn't stop this strange pull I feel toward him that lingers inside me. Him showing up here tonight tells me that he is interested in me but is holding back for some reason, and I want to know why.

On the way back home, Birdie cranks up the radio as the DJ continues to go on and on about some pop rocker who's gone missing, while my drunken brain tries to figure out the riddle that is Ace Johnson.

"They should try looking in every sleazy hotel around where he was last seen. The dude's probably on some two-week drug binge and doesn't want to be found." Birdie snorts in a fit of laughter as the radio starts playing an upbeat song by a band called Wicked White.

The repetitive lyrics of the song quickly get on my nerves and I turn the music back down, not able to handle the annoyance of a song I don't like in my drunken state. "I hate pop music. It has no soul."

Birdie laughs, instantly turning the music back up. "You think any song where the music overpowers the lyrics has no soul. Sometimes, Iris, music is just meant to be fun."

"Singing is a difficult talent to master, and the craft should be respected, not hacked to bits by synthesized drums created by a computer."

"Says the woman who dreams about being a singer on Broadway." She nags me all the time for being too picky musically, so her statement doesn't shock me. "You should lighten up and learn to have fun with music—to not take it so serious all the time—like this band, for example. They're relatively new on the scene but have already had like four or five songs on the radio. Are they memorable? No. But they're fun as hell to dance to."

I know what she's getting at, but music is special to me. When I discovered I had the gift of singing, it helped my self-confidence so much. People praised me for it, and in some weird way I felt like it would've made my mother proud of me too. So, needless to say, singing became serious business to me. It was important to perfect every note and feel every emotion in the lyric, which is why show tunes really grabbed hold of me. They all mean something. They tell a story. Not like pop music, where most songs are written to make money. Pop isn't written for the purity of conveying feelings.

"Let's agree to disagree." I lay my head back against the headrest in her Corolla and close my eyes as things around me begin to spin.

Ugh. I shouldn't have drunk so much. This is going to be so bad in the morning.

The next thing I know Birdie has the passenger door open and is nudging me awake as the dome light in the car assaults my eyes.

"How did you ever make it on your own in New York being a sloppy drunk like this?" Birdie complains as she helps me out of the car.

I lean against her as she walks me up the sidewalk and helps me fish the house keys from my front pocket. "I never drank there. New York is a tough city—nothing like here—and you always have to be on top of your game. Plus, I never wanted to be hung over if I ever got an unexpected callback."

A hiccup squeaks out of me and I sigh. "I just want to sing."

She laughs as I pull away from her and attempt to do a little spin to show her how good I'd be on stage, but my legs tangle together, causing me to fall backward.

A pair of strong arms hooks around me, halting me from hitting the ground. I close one eye and stare up at Ace's face to bring him into better focus. "Where'd you come from?"

He pulls me upright and attempts to stand me on my feet, but with the liquor coursing through my veins, I wobble and then fall back into him.

"Whoa, there." He wraps his arm around me as I lay my head against his chest.

It feels so nice being this close to him, and on top of it all he smells good enough to eat with his spicy scent. "You smell good."

Ace chuckles and the sound reverberates in his chest. "How much did you have to drink after I left?"

I glance up at his face with a goofy grin on my own. "So you were there."

He's hesitant at first, but then reluctantly nods. "I had to make sure you stayed safe. So I was there, and then moved when you saw me."

A gooey feeling of warmth envelops my chest at the thought of him wanting to take care of me yet again. Even though on the outside he seems to hate me with the passion of ten fiery suns because of how he's always so short with me, on the inside I think he likes me just as much as I like him.

I wrap my arms around his waist as I snuggle in closer to him, loving this confirmation of how he feels about me. I can't help myself. I'm so attracted to this man. It's nice to finally be able to touch him like this.

"I like you." My words come out like a dreamy sigh. "I wish you'd be this nice to me all the time."

I hiccup again and then close my eyes before Ace scoops me into his arms like I weigh nothing at all. I smile happily as I lay my head on his shoulder, feeling safe.

"Will you get the door for us?" Ace asks Birdie.

The sound of my keys jingling as she unlocks the door to my trailer catches my attention and I spot Birdie's concerned face. She doesn't trust Ace. I know she's thinking this is a mistake letting him take care of me like this, but she doesn't know how I feel about him. How much I crave this closeness.

"Which one is her room?"

"Down the hall—first door on the right," Birdie replies.

Light streams into my tiny room from the living area. The full-size bed in my room takes up 80 percent of the space, making it unbelievably tight, but it's what I've always known. That made living in my shoe box apartment in New York so easy. It was way more personal space for my things than I ever grew up with.

Ace lays me down on the bed, and the room spins. I throw my leg off the side of the bed, hoping it will ground me and give me enough balance to keep me from throwing up from motion sickness.

"Thank you," I whisper, grateful that he's been there so much for me today.

He smiles down at me and then stretches a tentative hand toward me, where he smooths back a few loose strands of hair from my face. "You're welcome."

When he turns to leave, the very thought of losing this magical connection scares me. I don't know if I'll ever get another moment with him like this.

Without thinking about the consequences of my action, I reach out and snag his wrist. "Stay."

"Iris . . ." The way he whispers my name makes my toes curl.

There's an edge to his voice that almost sounds painful, like for some reason he's torn whether to allow himself to give in to what I know that we are both feeling and stay here with me.

I don't want to push him away and ruin the progress we've made by being too forward, so I add, "Just until I fall asleep."

He scrubs his hand down his face and then sighs before his russet eyes meet mine. "Okay."

We stare at each other for a long moment, allowing me to study the contours of his handsome face. The definition in his cheekbones is enough to make any girl jealous while his nose brings balance, making his face masculine and rugged.

I reach up and trace the contours of his face with my fingertips. "You're beautiful."

He chuckles and shakes his head. "You've had a lot to drink."

I smile as I lick my bottom lip. "Yeah—but I still mean it."

I push myself up onto my elbows to closer inspect his face.

The stubble from a day-old beard covers his chin and scrapes against my fingers. "The perfect chin . . ." The tip of my finger runs down the center of his nose, feeling the slight bump in the middle—even that adds to his appeal. "Perfect nose . . ." I move on to his eyes and he closes the lids over them. "The most beautiful color . . ." Finally, I rub my thumb over his plump lips, fighting the temptation in my drunken state to find out what they taste like. "And the softest lips."

The lump in his throat bobs as he swallows hard, and his breathing picks up speed.

I lean into him, wanting more than anything to kiss him, only he holds back, pressing his forehead to mine. The man has unbelievable self-control.

"Iris . . ." It's a strained whisper.

He bites his lip, and just when I think his resolve is gone, Birdie's voice cuts in between us.

"Is she all right?"

Ace pulls away and turns toward the door. "Yeah. I think she'll be—"

Out of nowhere the amount of alcohol I ingested tonight decides to make a reappearance. The bile rises in my throat and I have no choice but to lean over the side of my bed and release the contents into the small trash can beside my bed.

"Oh, shit!" Birdie shouts and then gags. "I can't handle barf."

"Go ahead and go. I've got her," Ace orders.

"We don't know you. I'm not going to leave you alone with my friend," she yells in from the hallway.

"I'm not going to hurt her, I swear it." He turns back to me. "I'm going to get you a cold rag for your head and then get this mess cleaned up."

Heat rushes to my cheeks and I suddenly want to crawl into a hole somewhere with the thought that the man that I'm totally crushing on is going to clean up my puke.

I want to die.

When Ace leaves me, Birdie's voice carries into the room. "Swear to me that you're not some ax-murderer rapist, because if you so much as twist one hair on her head the wrong way, I will hunt you down and chop off your balls."

"Birdie!" I groan as I flop back onto my pillow. "Leave him alone. If he were going to kill me, he wouldn't be so hell-bent on taking care of me."

"He still needs to promise me," she shouts from the other side of the wall. "We don't know him."

"Love all, trust a few, do wrong to none," Ace tells her.

"Say what?" Birdie asks, confusion ringing through her voice.

Even I'm a bit confused by what he just said, but I let it go and chalk it up to just being really drunk.

"Never mind." He shakes his head as he reappears in the doorway holding a wet wash cloth. "No. I'm not an ax murderer. I'll take care of her. You don't have to worry."

He sits down next to me on the bed and then presses the cool cloth on my forehead. "This should help. Sleep. You'll feel better."

The bed coils lift me back up as he pushes himself off the bed. Birdie still stands guard outside my bedroom door with the look of concern etched on her face. Ace steps in front of her, meeting her stare head-on.

"Trust me," he says to her with a sweet voice.

There's a long pause before she finally sighs. Birdie makes eye contact with me, looking for confirmation that I'm okay with her leaving, so I nod and she gives me a halfhearted smile. "Call me if you need me."

"I will," I answer, allowing her off the hook as my protector as she heads to the front door.

My eyes dart to Ace, who grabs the garbage can and holds it away from his body as he leaves the room so he can dump the contents in the bathroom.

"Just leave it in there and I'll clean it tomorrow," I order.

I hear the toilet flush and then the water running in the bathtub, followed by the sound of the toilet flushing again. Ace quickly returns and sets the newly clean trash can back beside my bed. "All clean in case you need it again."

When his tall frame sits back next to me on the bed, the warmth of his body radiates off him, and it feels nice.

He readjusts the rag on my forehead. "Feeling better now?"

I lick my dry lips. "Believe it or not, throwing up helped. I don't feel as queasy."

"It usually does. Throwing up is your body's way of ridding the alcohol from your system."

"Had plenty of drinking experience, I take it?" I ask as I stare up at him.

Ace sighs. "Let's just say I've done my fair share of partying in my day, and the aftermath of a good time is something I learned the hard way."

I reach out and touch his wrist and then rest the palm of my hand on top of his as a thought occurs to me. "Tell me more about you. I want to know you."

Ace stiffens like telling me any bit of information about himself is the hardest thing he's ever had to do, but after what seems like an eternity of internal debate, he relaxes a bit. "There's not much to tell, Iris. I'm a relatively simple guy."

"I don't believe that's true. You're a complete mystery to me," I whisper.

He reaches out and traces his fingers along the lower portion of my jaw. "Why are you so nice to me? I've been a jerk to you. You should hate me, but you're always so nice to me. On top of that, I can't shake the feeling that you need me. All of that put together makes it impossible for me to stay away from you."

"I wish you would stop trying to," I say and mean it whole-heartedly.

"I don't know why you would want me after the way I treated you—the things I said—"

I press my finger to his lips. "These beautiful lips might've been harsh, but your actions showed you didn't mean them."

For the first time he smiles at me genuinely. "It doesn't seem like I'm that big of a mystery."

"You are to me."

He opens his mouth like he's about to say more but then quickly closes it and runs his fingers through his hair, mussing it and making it even more sexy. "I should let you get some sleep."

The mention of sleep alerts me to the fact that I'm exhausted. Sleeping on the way home from the bar isn't something I typically do, which is how I know I'm completely bombed. I need to sleep this liquor off.

Ace grabs the loose fleece blanket I keep at the foot of my bed and drapes it over me, tucking me in tight, leaning over me so close that we are nearly face-to-face.

Instantly, my eyes zoom in on his lips, wondering if he's going to kiss me because of the way he's looking at me, but I know because I just threw my guts up in front of him, that's not going to happen.

He bites his lip. "Good night, Iris."

I lick my lips and whisper the same thing to him before he pushes himself back and then heads out of my room.

I close my eyes and sleep.

CELEBRITY POP BUZZ NIGHTLY

The camera zooms in on Linda Bronson's smooth, angelic features as she brings the microphone up to her full lips. "We're here live with Wicked White's tour manager, Jane Ann Rogers, hoping to get to the bottom of where the band's front man, Ace White, has disappeared to."

Linda turns toward Jane Ann, who has on a tight leather jacket with trendy ripped jeans. "Jane Ann, can you tell us when the last time you saw Ace was?"

Jane Ann leans toward the microphone while her flaming hair frames her heart-shaped face. "The last time I saw him in person was when Ace walked off stage in front of twenty thousand people."

Linda brings the mic back to her mouth, poised to fire off another question. "Did you know his foster mother was ill?"

The redheaded woman nods. "Yes, and we're hoping that's what's at the root of his disappearance for the last couple of weeks. The thought of something tragic happening to Ace is unfathomable and not an idea that I even will entertain. We're hoping that wherever he is, that he's getting the closure that he needs and will be ready to come back and hit the road."

"Is it true that his bank accounts and cell phone have had no activity since his disappearance?"

"Yes, and that does concern us. If he's watching this report tonight, I'm begging him to at least call us and let us know that he's all right. I want him to know his Wicked White family and I are here for him."

Linda pats Jane Ann's shoulder with a look of sympathy plastered all over her face. "Our thoughts are with you. I think everyone in America can see how worried you are." She turns back to the camera. "There's a ten-thousand-dollar reward for information on Ace's whereabouts. If you or anyone you know have any information about Ace White's disappearance, you can call the LAPD. For *Celebrity Pop Buzz Nightly*, I'm Linda Bronson."

IRIS

The sun assaults my eyes the moment I roll over. Partying that hard is always painful the next day, which is exactly why I don't do it that often. I hate the repercussions of a good time.

I push myself up off my bed and my head immediately begins throbbing. Wrinkles form at the center of my forehead as I squeeze my eyes shut and pinch the bridge of my nose.

I'm never drinking again.

I sigh, dreading having to start the day with more cleaning and sorting of Gran's things. A hangover isn't exactly conducive to that type of thing, but I know I just have to put my big-girl panties on and get through it.

Even though I feel like death warmed over, a smile immediately erupts across my face as my eyes land on two ibuprofen tablets and a glass of water sitting on my bedside table with a note.

Ace's thick scrawl etched across the small piece of paper simply says "drink."

Who knew the asshole next door was so adorably sweet?

After taking the medication and forcing myself to eat breakfast, I get to work, headache and all.

Two hours after I begin sorting through Gran's clothes, I come across her favorite Sunday dress. Its blue-and-brown floral pattern stares back at me, reminding me of how great she looked when she wore it. She always seemed so happy every time I saw her in it, and it makes me think about how much her church family meant to her. While I was away in New York, the people from her church and her tenants here at Willow Acres were all she had.

It pains me that I took off in search of my own Broadway dream instead of spending more time with her while she was here. That's something I'll never get a do-over at, and more than anything I wish I could have one.

The front door of the trailer opens and Birdie's voice trails down the hall into the back bedroom where I am. "Iris?"

"Back here," I answer and then lay the dress I was just holding into the keep pile.

When she steps into the room, her eyes give me a once-over. "You look good, considering how rough your night was."

I shake my head, shuddering at the memory of throwing up in front of Ace. "It definitely wasn't my finest hour, but I'm feeling so much better."

Birdie sighs as she eyes the huge stacks of clothing I've strewn about the room. "Gee-Gee sure had a lot of stuff in this tiny place. How the hell did she fit all this stuff in here? This entire trailer can't be more than one thousand square feet."

"It's one thousand and thirty-nine, and Gran definitely knew how to pack every inch of this place full of stuff." I wink at her and then toss another dress in the donation stack.

She plops down on the bed and sighs. "I never realized how tiny these trailers were until I grew up. When we were little, there always seemed to be more than enough room."

I smile at her and nod, remembering clearly how we used to run through this place and Adele's next door. We never complained of being cramped. We loved being here.

Birdie watches me continue to sort through the clothing. "So what happened after I left last night? Did Sexy Trouble try anything funny with you?"

I laugh and shake my head. "No."

"Good. I was worried, you know."

I lay another dress down in the donations pile. "I seriously doubt you have anything to worry about when it comes to Ace. He was unbelievably helpful last night."

"Yes, he was. It takes a very special person to clean up someone else's vomit like he did. The man either has a stomach of steel or he's got it bad for you." She pauses for a long moment. "Did he say why he was at the bar last night?"

I frown, not wanting to repeat any of the intimate things that were said between Ace and me last night. "No, and I was too out of it to even think about asking him. Besides, he was being so helpful, I didn't want to be rude and seem unappreciative."

She sighs. "Helpful or not, I think it was weird how he was there last night but didn't bother to approach you. You need to get to the bottom of what's going on with him."

As much as I hate to admit that my overly paranoid friend is right, it was odd that Ace came to Angel's but never said a word to me, but later told me that I seem like I need him. I need to get to the bottom of all that.

"You're right. Now that I'm sober, I'll ask him about that the next time I see him."

This seems to appease her, because she gives me a curt nod. "Good, because I saw how the two of you looked at each other last night, and I think it wouldn't hurt to dig into his past before you go and do something crazy like fall for a man that you know absolutely nothing about."

"Who said anything about falling for him?" My stupid nose twitches, and I catch myself doing it.

Birdie cuts me off with a this-is-me-you're-talking-to look before I can say another word. "I know you, Iris. I know the look, plus your fucking nose is twitching again. Two words for you: Tanner Lawrence."

I cover my face with my hands and groan. "Oh, God. You know how I feel about mentioning him."

She grabs my elbows and pulls my hands away from my face. "I do, but I also remember how fast you fell for him back in high school only to find out what a rat bastard he really was right after graduation. I don't want you to invest your heart into some other creep without knowing what he's really like first."

I sigh. "Not every guy is going to screw every available woman within a ten-mile radius like Tanner did. Besides, relationships are built on trust—without that you have nothing."

"Still, promise me that you'll check him out before you go falling in love with him."

Her concern for me is sweet, and I love her for it, but I don't share her same suspicion of my sexy new neighbor.

After Birdie leaves to head to work, the rest of the afternoon drags on. Digging through Gran's closet both makes me smile and cry. On one hand it's nice to remember her, but on the other it guts me knowing that she's never coming back—that I'll never have another moment with her on this earth. That's what hurts the most, knowing that the one person who loved me more than anyone else is gone.

I glance over at the alarm clock on Gran's bedside table, and as if on cue, my stomach rumbles at the sight of it being almost two in the afternoon. I make my way into the kitchen and begin throwing ingredients into a pot to make myself some spaghetti. Just as the steam begins to waft through my tiny space, I notice Ace out front tinkering with his bike again.

The memories of how he took care of me last night flood my brain. He was so tender. I never pictured that from him at all. He took remarkably good care of me. He did the kinds of things Gran did for me when I was sick, and it was comforting having someone do that for me. It shows he cares, and makes me like him even more.

I owe him a huge thanks. Not many men would've done that.

The large package of pasta sitting on my counter causes an idea to spark, and before I can talk myself out of it, I march out the door toward Ace.

The noise from my door closing behind me draws Ace's attention. His russet eyes travel slowly down the length of my body as I approach him. It doesn't take a rocket scientist to figure out that the attraction I feel toward him is a mutual thing.

A wry smile dances across his lips. "You look much better today."

I bite my lip and toy with a loose strand of my dark hair. "Yes. Thanks to you."

"Me?" He raises an eyebrow. "I didn't do much."

I smile shyly as his gaze fixes on me. "I'd like to repay you. I want you to join me for a late lunch."

"I don't know—"

I hold my hands up, palm out to cut him off before he has the chance to refuse me. "Nothing fancy, I promise. I'm making spaghetti, and I always make enough for an army."

I see the hesitation in his eyes, so I add, "Please."

His eyes flick down to his grease-covered hands from working on his bike before he looks back up at me. "Okay, give me time to shower and I'll be over."

"Great!" I say a little too enthusiastically and immediately want to kick myself for being one of those overly excited girls. "It'll be ready in about twenty minutes."

I turn and practically skip back to my place, still enthralled by the fact that Ace is no longer being a major asshole to me. Last night was a total turning point for us for some reason. I'm not sure what I did or said from the time he came out to fix my lawn mower to when he helped me into the house last night, but I'm glad he's warming up to me.

Once I've prepared the food, I busy myself with setting two places just like I used to do for me and Gran. The small metal table with a yellow flowered top appears to be straight from the sixties, and knowing Gran, she'd probably had it since then too. It's so out-of-date, but I could never bear to get rid of it because this table is where we sat and had so many of our heart-to-heart talks.

A couple quick raps on the door cause butterflies to erupt in my stomach. The thought of being alone with Ace does something to my body physically.

I open the door, and there stands Ace, looking as mouthwatering as ever, freshly showered, in a clean T-shirt and jeans while his hair has been styled into a sexy mess on the top of his head. Just looking at that thick head of hair makes me want to tangle my fingers into it.

"Hi! Come in!"

Damn, Iris, tone it down, I mentally scold myself.

A crooked smile fixes on his face as he steps inside and then holds up a six-pack of beer with two of the bottles missing. "I think it's customary to bring something. This was the best I could do."

"It's perfect." I laugh as I take the cardboard container from him. I immediately hand him a beer and then pull one out for myself before putting the other two in the refrigerator.

Ace pops the cap off my beer and then his and tosses them in the nearby garbage can before he puts the bottle to his lips, taking a long pull from it. "This is really nice—a lot better than my place next door."

I smile at his approval of my childhood home as I sip my beer. "Thanks. My gran didn't have much, but she sure took pride in her home, making it look the best she could with what she could afford."

Ace steps toward the couch to get a closer look at the family photos hanging on the wall above it. I stir the spaghetti to busy myself with something so I don't just stand there staring at him. Never in all my life did I ever picture someone as hot as Ace Johnson would be standing in my living room.

He smiles as he points to my second grade school photo, where I'm smiling proudly without my two front teeth. "Cute."

I blush and let a small giggle escape. "That was Gran's favorite picture of me when I was little. She said that was my sweet phase."

His lips twist. "I don't know if I agree with that. I think you're still pretty damn sweet."

I feel more heat rise to my cheeks and instantly know that my blush has deepened at the sound of his complimentary words. Quickly, I try to change the topic, because if he keeps saying things like that, I might not be able to stop myself from jumping his bones. "I think Gran may have argued with you on that. She says the older I got, the more sassy I became."

He smiles at me, but it's not a happy smile exactly—more like one of those sad smiles someone gives you when they feel bad for someone. "Your gran sounds like she was a lot of fun. I can tell you loved her a lot. I'm sorry for your loss."

I swallow hard, trying not to cry yet again over the death of the one person I loved most in my life, so instead of elaborating, I simply reply with a faint, "Thank you."

I give the pot one last stir and try to change the subject. "I hope you're hungry."

"Starving."

After we fix our plates, we sit across from each other at the table.

Ace sprinkles some powdered cheese on top of the heaping mound of noodles, sauce, and meat that's on his plate. He moans and closes his eyes as he chews his first bite. "Iris, this is amazing. God, it's been so long since I've had a home-cooked meal. I forgot how good they are."

I bite my bottom lip, trying to reel in the huge, goofy grin that I know is blooming on my face. "I'm so glad you like it."

"Do you always cook this well? Because if you do, I might be tempted to hold you hostage at my place and make you cook for me."

I laugh. "That doesn't sound so bad to me."

Ace's jovial expression almost immediately disappears, and the smile drops off my face as well while I wonder what's going through that brain of his. "This is dangerous."

My pulse quickens at the sound of his words. "What is?"

His brow furrows. "Us—you and me. This won't end well, Iris, and you don't deserve that. You're too nice of a person—way too good for the likes of me."

"You can't possibly know that about me. Maybe you're too good for me. We don't even know each other that well to make those kinds of judgments." I sigh, utterly confused on why he keeps pushing me away. When he lets his guard down, we seem to get along so well together.

He shakes his head. "Everything I'm running from . . . it's not a life I would wish on anyone. It's selfish of me to hang around you.

You being around me could disrupt everything you've ever known if people associate you with me. I just feel like I need to look out for you."

His revelation causes my pulse to quicken beneath my skin. While he exposed his feelings for me, he still keeps the reasons he's dangerous all to himself. This causes my curious brain to go into overdrive as it starts developing theories on what exactly he's running from.

A long few beats of silence pass between us, and when I'm sure he's not going to divulge any additional tidbits of information, I ask in a soft whisper, "What are you running from, Ace?"

He picks up the bottle, his eyes never leaving mine as he finishes off its contents and sets it back down on the table. "I've got to go."

The moment he pushes back, I stand. "I'm sorry. I shouldn't have—"

He stands and holds his hand up, cutting me off. "It's fine, Iris, but I've got to go."

When he opens the door, I begin to panic, knowing that the connection we've been feeling is slowly slipping away. I stand in the open doorway as he makes his way down my front steps. "Ace, please."

"Thanks for dinner," he calls over his shoulder.

Those are the last words he says to me before he disappears around the corner and heads to his own trailer, leaving me to wonder exactly what this man is running from.

11

ACE

It's been two weeks since I spoke to Iris—nearly three since I walked off stage—and the dark-paneled walls of this trailer feel like they are about to close in on me. The two books I brought with me, I've already read at least five times each, and for the past two days I've done nothing but stare at the guitar I brought. It's been sitting there, taunting me to play again, so I finally give in and pick it up, enjoying the peace that strumming a familiar tune brings me.

Music has always been my one emotional release. It wasn't always easy talking about my feelings or how things were going in my life, and my mother understood that about me. She reached out to the broken little twelve-year-old the state dumped on her doorstep and encouraged my love of music.

While I would love to say that music instantly straightened me out and made me the reasonable man I am today, that's not exactly how it happened. It took a long time for me to mellow out. When I was younger, I had a lot of anger built up inside toward my biological mother, who left me stranded in a hotel room when I was just six so that she could run off with her pimp boyfriend. I used that aggression to lash out physically every chance I got to help ease the pain from the loss of the only existence I had ever known. Even though life with my biological mother kept me frightened most of the time, I was scared to be without her. She was the only constant in my ever-changing surroundings as we moved from place to place with whoever would take my mother and me in.

I didn't know it at the time, but my real mother leaving me in that room was the best thing that could've happened to me. Sure, it was rough bouncing from home to home until Sarah took me in, but at least I got fed and finally got the chance to go to school.

My fingers pluck at the strings as I close my eyes and allow my thoughts to drift, and I'll be damned if the very first thing that pops into my head isn't a vision of Iris. Her soft, smooth skin and flowing, thick brown hair only heighten her exquisite face. The green of her eyes and the natural pink pout of her plump lips draw me in every time, along with her long, toned legs. That body of hers is simply banging, and I'd give anything to be able to touch her the way I want.

She's everything I've ever dreamed about finding in my perfect woman, because coupled with her unbelievable beauty, she actually acts like she gives a shit about me—not my stardom, but about *me* as a person.

I shouldn't be thinking about her like this, but that doesn't stop me from wanting to whisk her into my world anyway.

Just as I begin to hum a melody that's flowing through my brain as I'm picturing Iris, I hear the unmistakable crank of an engine that's struggling to turn over. The racket is coming from outside, next to my trailer, which strikes me as odd because I didn't think Iris owned a vehicle that actually ran. Every time I've ever seen her leave, Birdie has been driving them somewhere in her little white Corolla.

Curiosity wins out and I set my guitar down and push up off the couch. Through the small window over the kitchen sink I spot Iris's sexy little ass as she leans over, checking the engine under the hood of what looks like a late-nineties Cavalier.

Without hesitation I take my opportunity to rescue her yet again in my lame-ass attempt to apologize for being a major asshole the last time we spoke. I've wanted to apologize but haven't been able to work up an excuse to talk to her again.

I have to stop turning into a complete fucking nutcase every time the girl starts asking questions. If I were her, I'd be curious as hell about me too. After all, I did come into this small little town, where everyone seems to know everyone, as a complete stranger. I guess I'm lucky that no one other than Iris has taken an interest in getting to know me better.

The gravel crunches under the soles of my black boots as I approach her. "You need a hand?"

She turns toward me. While I expect her to point a nasty scowl that I rightly deserve in my direction, I'm surprised by a sweet smile instead. "Do you know anything about cars?"

The tension I'm carrying in my shoulders releases and they instantly relax as I take another few steps to stand beside her in front of the car. "I do. For instance, to me it sounds like you've got a dead battery."

Iris rests her hip against the car as she stares up at me. "You could tell that from just listening to me try and start it?"

I smile at her and hold back a chuckle. Her lackluster knowledge of engines apparently extends to cars as well. "I could." I glance over at my bike and then flick my gaze back to Iris's face. "Do you have any jumper cables?"

She frowns. "I'm not sure. If Gran had any, they would be in the shed."

Iris pulls a set of keys from her pocket and singles out one from the ring before handing it to me.

I nod and then turn and head to the small ten-by-ten blue-and-white tin shed. The door creaks on its hinges as I pull it open. As soon as my eyes adjust to the dim light, I'm shocked by what I see.

It's not cluttered in here like I expected a shed would be. Walking in, I imagined random junk would be piled from floor to ceiling, but only the back wall has shelves, lined with boxes of items that are clearly labeled. The rest of the shed is lined with thick blankets, while a microphone rests on a stand in the middle of the small space. A karaoke machine sits on a small, wooden table.

I walk over and pick through the stack of CDs piled next to the machine, each containing music from Broadway musicals. I smile, loving the idea that Iris is into a more classic sound that focuses on the voice of the song.

"Did you find any cables?" Iris calls from the doorway.

I turn to look at her and find an odd expression on her face when she notices I'm going through her things, so I decide to just ask about what I've found. "You sing?"

She hesitates for a long moment and then nods. "Yes, but as you can tell, I only really sing one sort of thing."

I hold up the soundtrack of *Wicked*, and she smiles as she approaches me. "That's one of my favorites."

The curiosity of what her angel's voice would sound like singing flows through me, and I ask, "Would you sing for me?"

She bites her lip and the shy expression on her face causes my heart to race. Every time I think she can't possibly be any more attractive to me, she finds a new way to surprise and excite me, making her even more beautiful. "Okay."

She flips a couple switches, and red lights on the machine turn to green as a tiny screen lights up. "This little machine doesn't have the best sound, but it works. Gran got this for my seventeenth birthday—back when I decided being on Broadway was what I wanted to do after I graduated from high school."

"What happened with that dream?" I ask, trying to figure her out. "Did you ever give it a shot?"

She slides the CD into the slot and then works on selecting a track. "I did, or, well, still am, rather. I moved to New York a year ago after working for two years to save up some money, but came back here when Gran passed to get things in order."

I nod, remembering how not too long ago I set off to California in search of a music career as a soulful indie artist. Iris and I aren't so different after all. Matter of fact, it's almost as if we were cut from the same cloth.

I'm not sure where her parents are, but I've been around her long enough to figure out that they aren't in her life—that her grandmother raised her. So there's that, which we have in common, but we also both apparently really dig music, and not just any music, but music that almost takes on a life of its own—music that we can throw ourselves into and sing with every inch of our beings because we love it. In order to sing show tunes, you have to feel the music. Emotion is impossible to fake through them if performed well.

Iris sighs, pulling me out of my thought. "I started going to every open audition I could find. So far, I haven't had much luck, so I'm waiting tables until I can catch a break, but I know it's going to happen for me one day, because I'm never going to give up."

I smile, excited by her passion. "Well, let's hear it then."

"This one's my favorite. It's called 'I'm Not That Girl.'"

The music plays softly, and she steps up to the stand and licks her lips as she wraps her hands around the mic. Even though I don't know this particular song, the symphonic melody sets a dreamy atmosphere, and I already know she's about to blow me away before she even has the chance to open her mouth.

She takes a deep breath and closes her eyes like she can't bear to look at me while she sings. The moment the first word leaves her mouth, I smile at the buttery tone of her voice.

I was right. This girl is a fucking angel.

The pitch of her voice is perfect as she lands every note that the song calls for. I get lost in watching her perform this song, but I wish she would look at me. That's where I feel she's losing connection. If she does that when she auditions, it's the one thing holding her back from getting those parts she wants.

There's so much with the performance aspect of her singing I could help her with, but if I do that, I'll be opening myself up for a string of questions that I know inevitably will come—questions I don't think I'm ready to answer.

Finally, as she ends with the last note of the song, she opens her eyes to find me studying her intently.

A fierce blush rushes to her cheeks and she shrugs, like she doesn't know what to say under the scrutiny of my stare.

She bites her lip nervously. "Obviously, I still have a lot to work on . . . I'm self-taught, so my singing is still a work in progress."

I shake my head and, going against everything I just said I wouldn't do in my head, I step toward her, wanting to help. I want to tell her what I think she's doing wrong so that she can have a shot at her dream, even if that means I could out myself. Helping her also seems like a good way to apologize for being a dick.

"Iris . . . that was amazing. You've got so much talent," I praise.

Her green eyes light up with excitement like a child's do on Christmas morning. "You really think so? You're not just saying that?"

"No. I never bullshit about music. You've definitely got the chops for Broadway, it's just . . ." I hesitate, not wanting to hurt her feelings, but I know that in order for her to get better, she has to be told what she's doing wrong.

She lays her hand on my forearm. "Please, tell me. I can take it. Promise."

I stand beside her, so close that my chest nearly touches her shoulder. I'm itching to touch her, but I won't do it without permission. "May I touch you?"

She draws in a ragged breath and then nods. "Yes."

I curl the fingers of my right hand around her right shoulder and pull back a little so that her posture is perpendicular to the floor. At this angle, I can't help but notice her heaving chest and how her perky tits move in sync with each breath she takes.

I slide my left hand against her toned stomach and my pinkie grazes the warm patch of skin that's exposed between her T-shirt and the waistband of her jeans.

Our contact is fucking electric, and my own breathing picks up speed as I attempt to fight back the arousal I feel for her boiling beneath my surface.

"Everything about you is magnetic," I whisper in her ear, and she shivers at my words. "Don't be afraid to open your eyes and watch your audience enjoy you. Be confident and project. Let go."

I let go of her shoulder, and move to face her before pressing the repeat button on the machine. As the intro of the song plays, I say, "Do it again, but this time I want you to look at me."

This time when she opens her mouth to sing, when she begins to tip her head down, I slide my index finger under her chin and angle her head so that she's forced to peer into my eyes.

Her words are just barely above a whisper, so I slip my hand back on her abdomen and say, "Project—from here. Sing it like you mean it."

It's like lightning strikes this beautiful woman in my arms as she sings to me without fear. The words of the song come out effortlessly, and her voice could rival any of the greatest female vocalists of all time.

She's that damn stunning.

I nod approvingly and smile. "Yes!"

With that little bit of encouragement, she shocks me even more when she pushes herself to hit notes that are above and beyond what she reached the first time.

Only on the last lyric does she close her eyes while she holds the note there until the music stops. She releases a contented sigh as soon as the music ends, and when her beautiful eyes meet mine again, they swirl with emotion.

Completely blown away, I fumble with the words to tell her just how impressed I am. "Iris, that was—"

Without warning, she throws her arms around my neck and crushes her lips against mine. I know kissing her back is wrong, but I'll be damned if I don't want her so badly at this point that I can't stop myself from giving in. I've been so good with restraining myself when it comes to Iris, because protecting her from the chaos that I'll bring her is what's always been on the forefront of my mind.

Her fingers thrust into my hair, and I reach down and curl my hands around her thighs before hoisting her into the air. Instinctively she wraps her legs around my waist, and I thread one of my hands into her tousled curls while the other is busy cupping that perfect ass of hers.

"I've wanted you since you walked into my trailer," she breathes against my lips.

A thrill shoots through me at her admission of how long she's wanted me. "You've been driving me out of my mind from the moment I first saw you."

"Then take me." Her words leave her mouth in a breathy sigh as she gives me permission to ravage her body.

I've wanted her so much for so long, it would easy for me to say fuck it and give in and fuck her right here in this shed, but I know that's a dick move on my part. Iris Easton is not the kind of girl you can sleep with one time and never see again. She's the kind of girl that makes you change everything you thought you ever wanted in life just to be with her.

And I know for a fact I won't be living in Sarahsville long-term. If I want to keep avoiding Jane Ann and Mopar Records, then I have to keep moving, which means one day I'll leave this place *and* Iris behind.

Sleeping with her now, knowing that, would make me a fucking prick.

I pull back, breaking the lingering kiss we were just sharing, and sigh. "We can't do this, Iris."

A confused expression crosses her face. "Is it me? Did I do something wrong?"

I shake my head. "God no. It's me. I don't want to tangle you up with what's following me. I'm not looking to put down roots here, and I'll be leaving soon. I won't hurt you that way."

She blinks a couple times as she sets her feet back on the ground but leaves her fingers wound into the hair on my nape. "You can trust me, Ace. I like you. I want you. Whatever it is that you're running from—"

I cut her off. "Isn't your problem and I won't drag you into the crazy life I lead. Maybe someday when I get everything sorted out, I'll come back for you and we can try being together when everything calms down, but I don't know how long that will be. And I won't be a selfish bastard and ask you to wait while I figure it out. I don't want to make my issues your problem."

Tears drop out of her eyes and then roll down her cheeks. I'm doing exactly what I didn't want to do. I'm hurting her and it's killing me. I want to be with her. I want her to know the real me, but until I can figure out who the real me is now, I can't mix her up in my madness.

She pulls away from me, and I'm tempted to grab her wrist to stop her—force her to stay with me while I spill my guts out—but I'm afraid of how she'll react after finding out who I really am.

I don't want to lose the realness I feel with her.

So instead, I let her go while I watch the only person I care about walk away, hurt by me.

IRIS

I haven't spoken to Ace in over a week. Every time he's outside and I go out to talk to him, he walks away from me and either goes inside or jumps on his bike and speeds away, making it impossible for me to make him see that no matter what he's running from, we can work if he would give us a shot.

I know we can.

It's like every time we take a few baby steps forward, we tumble back down the ever-growing mountain he puts up between us. I'm not sure if the two of us will ever get over it at this point.

We've both admitted that we're attracted to one another, and we've both voiced how much we want to be together, but whatever Ace is hiding holds him back from allowing a relationship between us to progress.

I've been out in the shed every day since we kissed, practicing my posture and eye contact when I sing, just like he taught me. It's easy for me to remember how his hands felt on me—how electric his touch was, forcing the things he taught me to stay sharp in my mind.

I don't know how he knew how to fix my performance, but he did. The crazy thing is, he gave me tips like a professional would. He was totally comfortable performing, like he'd done it a million times before. He was able to instill confidence in me. He made me feel sexy, and the looks he threw me as I sang made me feel desired— wanted. That's why I couldn't keep from practically jumping his bones when I was through.

Even though he's back to avoiding me like the plague, Ace has still been doing things to help me, which shows me that he still cares about me.

He fixed Gran's car sometime during the night after we kissed. When Birdie and I went out to jump-start the car, we were shocked to see that we no longer needed to do that. I know it was Ace who fixed the car, because how else does a brand-new battery randomly show up in a nearly twenty-year-old car?

That man is exceedingly thoughtful. I just wish he'd let me in.

I sip the last bit of my morning coffee as an idea strikes me. When I was in New York and had Internet on my mini tablet, I could Google just about anything I wanted and find an answer. It's completely wrong of me to invade Ace's privacy like this, but I just have to know more about him. He acts like what he's hiding could hurt me, and if that's the case, maybe I should really heed his advice and leave him to his solitude.

I think about the tablet I have in my suitcase in my room, knowing there's no Internet connection available for miles around here, and just decide to do the easy thing and head back to the library to use their computer terminal.

After I get dressed, I make my way out to Gran's car and hop inside. The car cranks alive on the first try, and I carefully back out of the parking spot in front of my trailer and pull onto the street leading to the main road.

While driving, I sing some of my favorite show tunes to pass the time, since the radio in the car is broken and picks up only AM stations. I lift my chin as I sing one of my favorites from *The Phantom of the Opera* and remember to adjust the way I hold my body to reflect that I'm proud of the way I sing.

Once I park my car in the small lot in front of the library, I make my way inside and sit down at the first open terminal I see. I pull up a web browser and enter Ace Johnson into the search engine. Within seconds, millions of hits on Ace Johnson pop up. I begin clicking through the list, but each link leads me to a person who is not the Ace Johnson I'm looking for.

After going through two pages of links and not finding a social media page, mug shot, or anything on Ace, I decide to try clicking on the image tab to see what my search yielded.

I scroll down the sea of pictures, ready to give up, until a bearded man with similar features to Ace's catches my eye.

I click on the picture, and it leads me to a tabloid website with an article about that missing rock star that Birdie and I were talking about a couple weeks ago.

Celebrity Pop Buzz Nightly's report focuses on the mysterious Ace White, who has been missing since he stormed off stage before playing to a sold-out crowd in Detroit. It goes on to say that no one has heard from him since then. The last part of the article catches my attention.

"Any information regarding the whereabouts of Ace White can be reported to the LAPD. Mr. White's tour manager, Jane Ann

Rogers, is offering a ten-thousand-dollar reward for any information that leads to finding Ace White."

I lean back in the small swivel chair and stare at the screen, completely shocked by what I'm seeing. Is it possible that my new hunky next-door neighbor is this missing rock star, Ace White? The name fits, and the features, and banging body, but the man pictured in this article has long hair and a beard. It's possible it might not be him either.

Before I start jumping to some major conclusions, I open a new tab on the browser and search the name "Ace White." The first article I select shows Ace at a concert, singing from center stage and staring out to the crowd. His russet eyes are focused on the people he's singing to, and as I stare at his face, I know without a shadow of a doubt this is the man I've been pining over for the last few weeks.

This is what he's trying to protect me from? The media? There has to be something going on for him to walk away. I mean, he's living in my run-down rental when he can afford a swanky hotel. This man can have anything he wants. Why is he running from it?

Whatever it is, it must've been bad, and he obviously doesn't want to be discovered.

Everything starts to click now—his freak-outs when I question him about his past, how he knows so much about performing, the sexy way he carries himself, the vibe I got when I first laid eyes on him that he's far too good to be in a place like Willow Acres.

Quickly I close down my web browser before anyone notices what I've just been looking up, and I log out of the computer.

Despite the omission of the truth about his past, Ace is still someone I care a lot about, and if he doesn't want to be found, I'm going to help him keep his secret.

ACE

It's an unseasonably warm day in Ohio for November. Growing up here, fall was one of those times of year when it seemed like Mother Nature couldn't make up her mind if she wanted to freeze Ohio's residents to death or cause them to run up their electric bills by cranking up the air conditioning. Today seems like she's doing the latter.

Sweat drips down my back as the afternoon sun beats down on me. After a solid couple of weeks of mowing the grass around the trailer park, I'm finally on the last section of weeds.

After a couple more swipes I've managed to cut all the nearly knee-high grass around the place, and I feel good knowing that's the last time Iris will have to worry about it until next spring.

I cut the engine on the mower and then grab the hem of my T-shirt and bend to wipe the sweat from my face with it.

"Honey, come on over and get you a glass of lemonade. You've been working hard," an older female voice calls to me.

I glance up and notice a heavyset, gray-haired woman sitting under the metal awning attached to the front of her trailer. I guess you could consider it as being a porch. It's the trailer that I've learned over my short time here belongs to Birdie's grandmother.

The lady stands and goes to the pitcher sitting on the table next to her and grabs a red plastic cup from the stack sitting next to it.

When I don't immediately head toward her, she glances in my direction as she pours another glass of lemonade. "Well, come on."

"Yes, ma'am." I chuckle at her bossiness, and it reminds me of my mom and the way she never gave me a choice in the matter if she thought whatever she was ordering me to do was in my best interest.

The moment I approach her, she holds the glass out to me and smiles. Deep wrinkles set around her eyes and face tell me time hasn't been kind to her, but her pale blue eyes have a pleasantness about them. She's wearing a pair of worn jeans that appear to be so thin that they could tear any moment. The shirt she's wearing is the same way.

Even though she seems to practically have nothing, she's still willing to share with me what little bit she does have in the form of this homemade lemonade.

I smile as I take the cup from her. "Thank you."

I take a sip and her warm smile widens, clearly pleased that I'm enjoying my drink. "You're welcome. I'm Adele. I haven't had a chance to meet you yet, but I've heard good things about you from Iris."

I lift my eyebrows in surprise to learn that Iris still has nice things to say about me even though I treated her like a complete dick.

I don't reply to that statement from Adele and simply nod in response, but that doesn't stop her from going on.

"Iris is a good girl, stubborn, but good," Adele adds, and I laugh.

"I've noticed," I say as I smile and think about how persistent she has been with me.

Adele sits back down in the rocking chair she was in while I was out mowing and motions to the other wooden rocker beside her. "In my opinion there's nothing wrong with a woman to have some determination about her. Most people 'round here thought she was foolish for taking off to New York City to follow her dream, but not me. I'm downright proud of her for doing that—not allowing herself to get stuck in this little town like the rest of us did."

She sighs. "I envy that she was brave enough to do that. I wish I had her guts when I was her age. Maybe then I would've seen more of the world than just what Ohio and West Virginia had to offer."

"You've never been outside of those two states?" I ask, amazed that she's allowed herself to be confined so much her entire life.

Adele shakes her head. "Nope. I was born in West Virginia and I met Earl when I was just fifteen, got married when I was sixteen, and we moved here to Ohio so he could get a job. I've been here ever since, but I don't regret putting roots down. There's a lot to be said about knowing people in the place you live. Take Iris's grandma, for example. Gee-Gee and I were the best of friends since I moved here in the late seventies after Earl passed. We helped each other raise our girls, and then when they each had a girl of their own and decided they no longer wanted to stick around and be mothers, we raised their kids."

I take another drink as my curious brain begins wondering if Iris's mother was like mine—too into partying to be a mom. "Whatever happened to Iris's mom?"

Adele curls her fingers under the front of the armrests as she continues to rock in a slow, steady rhythm. "She passed when Iris was about six from a drug overdose. They found her in a bathtub in a hotel somewhere in Florida.

"I worried about Iris for the longest time. Poor thing was heartbroken over her mother. I just thank the stars above that Gee-Gee had already been raising Iris from the time she was in diapers or she might not've turned out so great. That can really mess a kid up, you know, watching your mother sink into a downward spiral."

Isn't that the truth? I know far too well about that scenario.

Adele waves her hand dismissively. "Enough about all that sad stuff. I want to know more about you. Where're you from and what's your story?"

I laugh, knowing there's no way to get around giving this direct old woman information. "I grew up in Columbus. I didn't have a biological mother either, she was a lot like Iris's mom, I guess, but thankfully I was removed from her care and eventually placed with the woman I consider to be my mother."

"Ah." She nods. "A foster family. How'd that work out for ya?"

I shrug. "At first I was sent to live with some people who simply looked after orphaned children for the money and didn't have their best interests in mind. Those homes—they weren't pleasant in the least, but when I was twelve I met Sarah, and she was the first person who ever took an interest in helping me cope with the loss of my biological mother and refocus my emotions in a positive way."

"How'd she do that?" Adele asks.

"By showing me that I was an intelligent kid with a future, and she also pushed me to discover my creative side."

Adele smiles, clearly pleased with my answers. "So you're attractive, smart, *and* an artist. I can see why our little Iris has taken a shine to you. If I were a few years younger . . ." She cackles. "You should do right by her, you know. She's a good girl."

"I know that," I say in a low voice. "That's why I'm keeping my distance. I don't want to hurt her."

"Son." Adele leans forward and pats my knee. "You'll hurt her more if you don't tell her how you feel and give whatever's going on between the two of you a chance."

My lips pull to one side as I consider what she's saying. Maybe she's right. I do want to be with Iris more than anything right now. She may accept the fact that I've hidden my identity from her fairly easily. Hell, she might even be okay with going on the run with me if Jane Ann and the media get too close on my trail. She might be willing to be my Bonnie if I ask her.

It's almost as if just by sitting here with Adele and talking, I see things a little clearer. I need to open up with Iris, tell her about me, and then give her the chance to decide for herself if she can handle everything that comes with being with me.

Just then I spot Iris in the window of her trailer, watching me as I sit next to Adele. There's an odd expression on her face, like she's doing more than just looking at me. It's more like she's studying me . . . like she's seeing me for the first time.

I haven't spoken to her since that day out in the shed. She doesn't deserve to be treated like that, but I know that if I get too close to her again, I won't be able to maintain my resolve.

A shiny, black older-model BMW pulls up out front of Iris's and Adele's trailers and honks the horn, jerking my attention away from the conversation I was just having. A tall, broad-shouldered man wearing a tan suit gets out of the driver's side and then buttons his jacket with one hand and raises the other in greeting when he spots Adele and me sitting outside.

"Hi, Tanner! How are you?" Adele waves back and then whispers to me, "I can't stand that little snake."

I hold back a laugh as Adele continues to smile at the man, because I don't want to give away her true feelings about him.

"I'm great, Adele. You look fantastic." He points to Iris's place. "Is she home?"

I fight the urge to roll my eyes. I can tell from a mile away that whoever this dickhead is, he's as fake as a fucking three-dollar bill.

"I'm not sure," Adele replies, but we both know Iris was just watching us through the window.

For whatever reason, Adele isn't willing to give this guy info like she just did me. Must mean she likes me.

Just then, Iris walks around her trailer. The sight of her nearly steals my breath every time. She's not wearing anything fancy, just her typical jeans and T-shirt, but I'll be damned if she doesn't make it the sexiest outfit known to mankind.

The woman looks great in anything she wears.

"Iris," Mr. Fake says with a sly grin on his face, and I'm not sure if it's the abundance of gel in his dark hair or the grin that makes me determine he's a prick, but I've already made my judgment about him. "Wow. You look . . . wow. It's so good to see you."

Iris folds her arms across her chest. "What do you want, Tanner? I thought I told you I didn't want to see you again."

"Baby . . ." Tanner takes a step toward Iris and my back stiffens.

The thought of this guy touching her is enough to make me grit my teeth. Adele must sense it, because she pats my knee again and whispers, "Stay calm. She'll handle him. Stubborn, remember?"

I give her a small nod and attempt to relax in my seat with no luck. When it comes to Iris, the protector in me gets out of control really quick. I'm not sure if it's because in my heart of hearts I know I'm the one who's meant for the job or if it's because I know for a fact that she's alone on this earth like me.

"Don't *baby* me. *You* don't get to call me that." Iris holds up her hand and Tanner stops in his tracks. "You have exactly five seconds to tell me why you're here before I call the cops and file a restraining order."

Adele cackles beside me, delighted by Iris's feistiness, and it makes me smile too.

He rubs the back of his neck. "Jesus, Iris. I said I was sorry about before. Aren't you ever going to forgive me?"

"No. You're an asshole. Two seconds, Tanner," Iris warns.

He sighs. "I did come on business. I'm the new county tax auditor, and Gee-Gee was nearly four years behind on paying the property taxes on Willow Acres. I hate to be an asshole, seeing as how you just inherited the place, but it's my job to tell you that you have thirty days to get them paid before the state begins the process to take possession of the property."

"They can't do that!" Iris argues. "I need more time than that."

Tanner frowns. "If I could give you an extension, I would, Iris. You know how I feel about you."

"Damn it," Iris grumbles as she shoves her hand into those thick, flowing locks of hers and pushes them away from her face. "Where would all these people go? Tanner, please. You know I'll figure out a way to pay it. How much is it in total?"

"It's twenty thousand dollars, Iris. There's no way you can come up with that."

Adele gasps beside me while grasping at her chest and staring up at the sky. "Oh dear Lord in heaven. How could you not tell me it was that bad, Gee-Gee?"

The thought flows through my head. Twenty thousand would save this place? I could go withdraw the money from my account, but I know as soon as I do, Jane Ann will have her spies everywhere and she'll find me in no time.

But if Iris and the good people like Adele who live here need it in order to keep their homes, I'll do it.

Iris scrubs her hands down her face and Tanner wraps his fingers around her wrists and pulls them away. Instantly, I feel the jealous twinge that he gets to touch her when I can't. "Iris, come to dinner with me. We'll talk things over and figure this thing out together."

She jerks out of his hold. "Don't *ever* touch me again. You lost the right to do that when you decided you couldn't keep it in your pants. There will never be a 'we' or a 'together' involving us ever again, Tanner. *Never.* Get that through your head. When I said I was done, I meant it. I've moved on."

My jealousy turns to absolute selfish delight when I hear her speak those words, because I can't help but be elated that maybe it's me she's talking about moving on with.

Tanner swallows hard. "Fine. But you don't have to make it so rough on yourself, Iris. Call me when you come to your senses and want to take me up on my offer to help."

"Never going to happen. Now, leave." The stern expression she's wearing could rival any hardball music mogul who is trying to negotiate a deal any day, and I love it.

But above all else, I feel there's still hope that she'll give me a second chance to prove that she can trust me. I want to be the one that she allows to help her.

Chapter
14

CELEBRITY POP BUZZ NIGHTLY

The camera zooms in on the program's top field reporter, Linda Bronson. Her golden hair flows in the delicate breeze as she stands in front of a skyscraper in downtown Columbus, Ohio. "Good evening, I'm Linda Bronson, reporting to you live from Columbus, Ace White's hometown. As many of you already know, Mr. White has now been missing for well over a month. The reward for information leading to discovering where Mr. White may be has now been doubled by his tour manager, Jane Ann Rogers."

The television show begins flashing several pictures of a bearded, long-haired Ace White and then flashes to a press conference being held by the chief of police at the LAPD.

"As Chief Wolfe stated in the conference he gave earlier this week, finding a missing person a month from their disappearance becomes a hard task. At this point everyone involved is fearing the worst. Many believe Ace White has met an untimely demise since there's been absolutely no activity on his credit cards or cell phone. This has been called one of the most intriguing cases since Jimmy Hoffa went missing.

"I want you all to rest assured that I'm not going to give up. I'm going to keep turning stones until something pops up. For *Celebrity Pop Buzz Nightly*, I'm Linda Bronson."

Chapter
15

IRIS

I stand in the road, still steaming mad as I watch the pricy BMW pull out of the trailer park. I can't believe Tanner Lawrence had the nerve to not only show his face here, but had the audacity to ask me out on a date after the way he screwed around on me right after high school.

Asshole.

"You handled that well, honey," Adele calls from the rocker, her usual seat when the weather is nice. "Gee-Gee would've been proud of the way you stood up to him."

I smile at her. Gran and Adele never liked Tanner. Oh, I suppose they tolerated him for my sake, but they certainly didn't enjoy his company. Gran told me after I broke it off with him that she thought he was a dirty snake and was glad I discovered how he really was before I did something crazy like marry him or get knocked up by him one day.

I wonder what Gran would've thought about Ace? I bet she would've liked him.

My eyes flit to Ace, who appears to be overly chummy with Adele, which is odd, considering Adele really doesn't like anyone and does her best to keep to herself. Gran was about the only person who ever visited Adele, with the exception of Birdie's mother, who would stop by from time to time to bum money off her, and Birdie once she got her first job at sixteen.

I debate going over to hang out and chat with Adele to get some advice from her until I've cooled off, but with the way Ace has been ignoring me for the past week, I think I'd better not, since he's sitting over there and I just might lay into him too.

I take a step backward and Ace frowns at me like he's disappointed that I'm not coming over.

"I'll see you later, Adele," I say.

Ace leans forward in his chair, and for a moment it appears that he might be coming after me, but he stops the moment I shake my head slightly to discourage him.

I'm too worked up over this whole tax situation with Tanner, and I don't need Ace around right now, reminding me of how he rejected me.

I need time alone—time to think.

The rest of the afternoon and into the evening I busy myself with sorting the last of Gran's things. I tape the last cardboard box full of clothes shut just as there's a knock on the door. I glance up at the clock on Gran's nightstand. It's time for Birdie to be getting off work, so I'm sure it's just her coming to hang out as usual.

"Come in," I call from the back bedroom. "I'm in Gran's room!"

"Iris?" Ace calls.

I gasp and catch a glimpse of my sweaty face in the mirror on Gran's dresser.

Shit!

I look like hell.

Quickly I work on smoothing down the unruly curls that have sprung out all around my face. "Be right out."

Oh my God. What's he doing here?

As my pulse quickens beneath my skin, I hurry out of the bedroom and down the hall, trying to figure out what he could possibly want.

The minute my eyes land on Ace, my heart does a double thump against my ribs.

He's got on those expensive-looking jeans again that hug his sexy backside perfectly, and a tight T-shirt that shows off his toned chest. Could this man be any more stunning?

He holds up a pizza box and a six-pack of beer. "I brought the peace offering this time. It's not cookies . . . but . . . I figured this could work, since I don't bake for shit."

His eyes meet mine and he chews on the corner of his lower lip like he's worried I might tell him to take a hike. While I should be angry with him for the way he walked out on me and then ignored me, I can't. I like him too much. Now that I know his secret, I understand why he's fighting so hard to keep me at bay. He doesn't want to be found out for some reason, so I can respect his decision to push me away, even though I wish I could tell him that he doesn't have to—that he can trust me.

"Great. I'm starving." I smile at him, and the worried expression morphs into a lopsided grin.

I walk past him and head straight for the kitchen, where I wash my hands and then open the cabinet that holds the plates. I grab two and set them on the table.

After we each put a slice on our plate and open a beer, I ask, "What were you and Adele talking about earlier? You two looked chummy."

Ace takes a bite and grins as he swallows it down. "You, actually."

I raise my eyebrows, shocked by how easily he admitted to talking about me, but now my stupid curiosity is piqued. "What about?"

He shrugs. "About your mother—how you went off to New York, how she hates Tanner. You know, basically your whole life story."

My mouth gapes open. Damn. I guess Adele was just a wealth of information for him, and that isn't like her.

I push the pizza around on my plate. "If you wanted to know something about me . . . why didn't you just come and ask me?"

I know that isn't a fair question, seeing as how I just Internet stalked him, but I would've answered any question he asked me openly. Unlike him, I have nothing to hide about myself.

He shrugs. "I didn't go prying, if that's what you're thinking. Adele just told me all of that stuff."

Ace is quiet for a moment, and then he asks, "What's going on between you and that Tanner guy? Are you seeing him?"

"No!" I blurt. "God no. He was my boyfriend back in high school and for about six months after until he decided he wanted to start screwing every coed on campus that would have him when he went off to college."

"I see." He nods, like the little show Tanner and I put on in front of him and Adele now makes sense.

He takes a long pull from his beer, and I can't help but notice the way his sexy mouth works against the bottle. It causes a shiver to run down my spine, remembering how his lips felt on mine and how electric we seemed to be together.

"Iris . . . about us." His russet eyes meet mine, and I see nothing but sincerity in them. "I want you to know, that what happened in the shed—"

"Please," I whisper, not wanting to hear his reasoning why we can't be together yet again. "You don't have to apologize. I shouldn't have been so forward. I kissed you. I started it. I should be the one apologizing to you, but I can't say I'm sorry that it happened."

I wish I could just come out and tell him that I already know what he's hiding. I don't care why he's running from his life, because his career isn't him, he's got the right to decide if he wants to quit.

I want him to know that nothing will change the way I feel toward him—the desire I have for him has nothing to do with his fame, if that's what he's worried about. I lusted after him before I found out who he was.

He reaches across the table and threads his fingers with mine. It's a small gesture but an intimate one, and it immediately makes me smile. "I've been pushing you away since I got here, and I'm sorry. It's just I'm so insanely attracted to you that I know once I have you, it'll be all over for me. Today, just watching that guy beg you to go out with him—it made me so fucking jealous. I wanted to tell him to take a fucking hike because you weren't available, but I didn't have the right."

"He's not the one I want," I say, hoping he will catch the hint in my voice.

An expression of relief floods his face as his eyes soften. "Good, because I've decided I have to figure out a way to make you mine."

The beautiful admission coming from his mouth causes a swarm of butterflies to take flight in my belly.

I bite the inside of my bottom lip but then allow the goofy smile I'm trying to hide shine through. "You did?"

He brings our interlaced hands to his face and he kisses my knuckles. "Yes. I'm willing to do whatever I have to do in order to be with you."

I reach up and stroke the side of his face with my fingers, and he closes his eyes and leans into my touch, clearly enjoying the comfort of it. I need to try to make him understand that what he's hiding . . . it doesn't scare me. "I don't care what it is you're running from, Ace. I'll be with you anywhere. I'm yours."

In one swift movement Ace is up on his feet, pulling me with him. He yanks my body flush with his and wraps his strong arms around my waist. I sigh as I melt into him, overwhelmed that I'm finally getting what I want: him.

Both of his hands glide up my back before he brings one around to trace the line of my jaw with his index finger. "Stunning."

That's all I manage to let him say before I attack him with my lips. There's no resistance in his kiss this time. He cups my face and his greedy tongue seeks entrance into my mouth. I part my lips, allowing his hot, slick tongue to slide against mine, and they begin their sensual dance of foreplay.

Every nerve inside me is alive with need for this beautiful man before me. It's not just his amazingly good looks that turn me on, but how he's been there for me the past few weeks, helping me whenever I seem to need it the most.

My fingers walk their way up the coarse material of his jeans and then slip under the hem of his T-shirt to play with the soft skin on his waist.

A low grunt sounds in the back of his throat and he yanks my hips into his even more, allowing me to feel the growing erection inside his jeans against my belly. Turning him on like this excites me. I throw my fingers into that beautifully messy head of bronze hair and continue to kiss him.

He pulls back and kisses a fiery trail across my cheek to my jaw before he kisses the tender flesh below my ear and then whispers, "You smell fucking delicious. I can't wait to taste you."

Oh. My. God.

I nearly combust right there on the spot as my toes curl at just the thought of having Ace's face between my legs. I squirm against him as my panties grow wet with my own arousal.

Just like in the shed, Ace reaches down and hoists me up so that my legs wrap around his waist, and he begins walking us over to my couch. I unwrap my legs and stand before him as he backs up against the couch. Unable to wait any longer, I grab the bottom of his shirt and whip it over his head in one swift motion. My eyes follow the long, lean muscles in his chest down to the incredible set of drool-worthy abs on display in front of me. Most rock stars I've ever seen pictures of are covered in tattoos, but surprisingly, Ace only has one. It's a line of script above his heart.

I run my fingers over the words and read them aloud. "'To thine own self be true'?"

He smiles. "It's a quote from my favorite Shakespeare play, *Hamlet*. It's a reminder to me to always put myself first."

I smile seductively. "How'd you become so knowledgeable about something so romantic?"

"Let's just say I'm more than a pretty face."

He laughs and I wrap my arms back around his neck, giggling along with him. I toy with the hair at his nape, loving the way it feels between my fingers. "Kiss me."

His playful smile grows serious and his eyes flood with desire after hearing my request. "Happily."

The caress of his hands as they grip my hips and yank me to him feels amazing. How I've longed for him to hold me like this—need me like this—want me like this.

When our lips meet again, the warmth of his kiss nearly sends me over the edge. Eagerly I meet every thrust of his tongue inside my mouth with a moan that I can no longer hold back. This feels so good—he feels so good—so right.

I shudder when his fingertips find the bottom of my shirt and his pinkie grazes the skin across my back.

"I want to see you," he whispers before he slides his hands up my torso, bringing my shirt up along with them.

The moment my shirt comes over my head, he lowers his head and kisses my exposed shoulder. His calloused fingers caress my bare skin before his right hand tangles itself into my bra in the back and unhooks it.

Ace stares into my eyes as he takes his sweet time torturing me with his gentle touch, slowly pulling each strap down, allowing my white lace bra to fall at our feet.

No man has ever had this much self-control with me, and it's absolutely killing me slowly.

His tongue darts out, and he leans in and licks my top lip before he presses his lips to mine yet again. "Exquisite."

I love hearing him speak. I love the sweet, romantic words that flow from his mouth, and greedily, I want more. "Do you know any more lines from Shakespeare?"

"I know plenty," he murmurs against the soft, sensitive skin below my ear.

I toss my head back to give him better access as he works his way down my neck. I gasp the moment he sucks one of my nipples into my mouth. Careful to give my other breast the same attention, he flicks his tongue across the taut skin as he works the button of my jeans loose, and then the zipper.

When he kneels down, he stares up at me adoringly. "Lift your foot."

I do as he orders, and he removes my Converse sneaker and then motions for me to repeat the action with the other foot. Once that's done, he works the stiff material of my jeans down my hips, pausing to kiss my stomach just above my underwear before removing those as well.

Standing there on display for him, I should feel self-conscious as his eyes roam over me, but I don't. The way he's staring at me with his desire-coated eyes—it makes me feel powerful, and sexy. I love that I do that to him.

He lifts my left leg and sets my foot on the seat of the couch and traces a finger down my wet folds. "Perfect," he says as he stares up at me adoringly, and I shiver.

The first tender touch of his tongue against my flesh causes me to suck in a quick breath as I grab a handful of his hair. His eyes dart up to my face and we make eye contact while he continues to roll his tongue against my throbbing clit.

I've never had anybody look at me with so much intensity before, especially while pleasuring me, but I like it.

It's so damn hot.

After I'm dripping wet, he slides a finger inside me and begins working me into a frenzy as he continues to pump and suck at my most sensitive flesh. Soon a familiar tingle erupts through me and I tense, not ready to give, but not able to stop it either.

"Oh, Ace," I cry out as I come hard against his mouth, and he continues to lap at my juices.

He sets my leg down on the ground and stands and wraps me in his arms until the shudders subside. I rest my head against his chest and sigh contentedly but find that I'm still hungry for him.

I don't think I'll ever get enough of him.

I lean back and kiss his lips, tasting my own arousal on him.

"'Hear my soul speak: the very instant that I saw you, did my heart fly to your service,'" Ace says against my lips, and it takes every inch of self-control I have to not attack him with my lips instead of allowing him to take his time with me.

Now it's my turn to please him.

I make quick work of yanking his jeans down and then find myself staring at the huge bulge in his boxer-briefs. I bite my lip as I slide my hands into the waistband and then work them down over his hips.

His cock springs free, hard and at full attention, and I lick my lips as I nudge him back until he sits on the couch. I kneel before him and remove his boots and clothes, and then push myself between his knees.

He reaches up and tucks his index finger below my chin before running his thumb across my lips. I suck his thumb into my mouth and it sets his eyes ablaze with lust. "Let me please you."

I grab the base of his cock in my hand and stroke it one time. His mouth drifts open as he watches me touch him, and it turns me on knowing I'm turning him on.

I tuck my hair behind my ears and then lean in, taking the tip of him in my mouth. I swirl my tongue around the ridges of his head, and he gasps.

"Holy fuck!" he whispers loudly and then lays his head back. "Jesus. You can't keep doing that. I'll come. I've wanted you too long. I won't last."

I smile devilishly as I suck him as far into my mouth as I can without gagging myself. I only pump him in and out a few times before he taps my shoulder and says, "Not like this. I want to be inside of you the first time."

I pull back and nod, agreeing because I'm still so turned on that I'm not done with him yet. My body craves him—needs him inside of me.

He reaches down and grabs a foil package from the pocket of his jeans, and I raise an eyebrow. "Expecting to get lucky tonight?"

He chuckles as he rips the package. "Not expecting, but hoping."

I laugh as I take the condom from him, and things turn serious again the moment I touch his cock and begin rolling the thin sheath down his thick shaft.

Ace guides me to stand up and then to straddle him on the couch. The moment his cock slides against me, I rock my hips a few times to coat him in my arousal.

I groan into his ear as he pulls my chest against his and holds me tight. He raises his hips and thrusts once, and the tip of him enters me. My fingers curl into a fist, clinging to him as he allows my body to adjust to his considerable size.

"'This is the very ecstasy of love,'" he whispers in my ear and then sucks a quick breath between his teeth as he pushes all the way inside of me. "'Such is my love, to thee I so belong, that for thy right, myself will bear all wrong.'"

I moan as he presses his cheek against mine, and I allow myself to get lost in the essence of him.

I close my eyes as I rock my hips in time with his. Each thrust, coupled with the sweet lines he's whispering in my ear, stokes the coals of desire smoldering in my core.

I buck wildly, searching for my release, and he digs his long fingers into my hips. "Jesus, Iris. I don't know how much longer . . . fuck."

Loving that he's losing control, I pump faster, wanting him to get lost with me. Warmth spreads through me, and I cry out, gripping a handful of his hair as I come even harder than I did only moments before.

"Ahh . . . Iris," he groans as his body grows rigid and he comes.

I watch in awe as this man below me lets go and his face contorts in pure pleasure.

I collapse against him and he traces light circles against the bare skin on my back.

"That was . . ." I sigh contentedly, so relaxed I can't even finish a coherent thought.

"Phenomenal," he finishes for me, and we both laugh.

I pull back so I can gaze upon his breathtaking face, and then I push a loose strand of his bronze hair off his forehead. "That was pretty amazing."

He gives me an adorable smile. "*You're* amazing."

I lean in and kiss his lips and correct him. "*We're* amazingly perfect."

We lie there, still attached as one, enjoying each other for a while, kissing and caressing each other's bodies. When he pulls out of me to discard the condom, I immediately miss his warmth but am pleased when he rushes back from the hallway with the blanket from my bed in his hands.

Ace lies back down beside me, putting me between the couch and his side before throwing the blanket on top of us. I hook one leg over his and rest my head against his chest. I absently trace patterns across his toned chest while reliving what he just did in my head.

What happened between us just now was clearly more than casual sex. Those quotes . . . they were the some of the sweetest words I've ever heard. It's hard to fathom that this very sensual man feels that way toward me. It blows my mind.

"What are you thinking about?" His voice rumbles in his chest.

I sigh, not wanting to admit what's on my mind, but also wanting him to open up to me. "Why me?"

His thumb absently strokes my shoulder, and it feels nice. "At first, I'll admit, I was drawn to your looks, and that pissed me off."

I giggle and snuggle in tighter. "You were mean to me because you liked me? That makes it sound like we're in the second grade."

He chuckles. "I suppose it does. I was a complete asshole to you and I apologize. You did nothing to deserve my animosity."

"But you didn't like me much at one time?" I ask, unsure if I really want to hear the answer to that, but I know I need to.

"Yes," he says simply. "I didn't want to be caught up in anything, and you . . . I knew if I allowed myself the chance to get to know you, that I would be hooked. I wouldn't ever want to leave you if I had you like this, and I was angry that you were making me want to stay and abandon all my plans for a life on the road."

"What changed your mind?" I ask, questioning his sudden change of heart.

He tips my chin up so he can gaze upon my face. "It was impossible for me to stay away from you. Your beauty drew me in, but the way you looked at me, like you wanted to know the real me . . . it sealed your fate. You and I . . . we're kindred spirits. We have a lot in common."

I nearly laugh, knowing that his lifestyle and mine are completely different. Then guilt hits me for keeping silent about the fact that I know his secret.

It would be so much easier between us if he would just come out and tell me who he is. Then I wouldn't have to pretend that I don't know.

Maybe if I hint around . . .

"Can I ask you something?"

"Anything," he replies as he stares down at me with a smile on his face.

"How did you know how to help me with my singing?"

His body below me tenses. "About that . . . there's something I need to tell you about me. You might not like it . . . and I'm not sure how you're going to react, but I need to be up-front with you about who I really am and what I'm running from."

"Ace . . . I don't—"

He holds up his hands. "Just hear me out, because I want you to understand me and why I may need to leave again one day without much notice."

"Ace, I know who you are," I say, wanting to put him out of his misery about having to explain something I already know.

He sits up, pulling me up with him. A panicked expression flashes in his eyes as he fixates his stare on me.

My heart races, and suddenly I'm afraid of making him angry with me for snooping around about him, but I know if we're to ever have any type of real relationship between us, then we shouldn't keep secrets from one another.

"Please don't be upset with me. Last week, after you pushed me away, I had to know why. I had to know what you were running from—what was so bad that you had to protect me from yourself. I wanted you, more than anything, and I knew you wanted me too, but you wouldn't allow yourself the chance, and I had to know *why*.

"So, I drove to the closest library and used their computer to look you up."

There's an incredulous expression on his face, but he still hasn't said a word, and the suspense of not knowing what he's thinking is killing me. "Say something, please."

Ace rakes his hand through his sexy mess of hair on the top of his head and lets out a ragged breath before meeting my gaze again. "You aren't pissed at me for lying to you about who I am?"

I shake my head. "No, because I'm pretty sure I got to know Ace Johnson pretty well over the last month. You can introduce me to Ace White slowly."

He shakes his head. "You don't need to know Ace White. He's a fucking poser and I hate him."

I frown, not liking the way he's speaking about himself. "Ace . . . he's a part of you. Don't say that."

"But it's true, Iris. None of what Ace White does is me. It's all an act. It's not my kind of music, clothes, or even the fucking hair-style—the record label that discovered me . . . that was all part of my contract. I signed it because I thought it was my big break and that someday Mopar Records would give me a shot to become the artist I really want to be. Singing this lame-ass pop rock that I didn't have any creative input on isn't me."

I reach over and thread my fingers through his. "Is that why you left?"

He shrugs. "That's part of it. No one in that business gives a damn about me. I was just a voice and a face to them, not a person. They discounted my feelings and, well, it was the tipping point when my foster mother, Sarah, was on her deathbed and they wanted to stop me from going to her because I had scheduled shows. She was the only person in this world that ever took the time to love me—to care about me. I was going to be damned if I put people who didn't give a shit about me before her, so I left—just walked out and walked away from everything. I was tired of killing myself to make everyone around me rich while making myself miserable."

My heart squeezes in my chest. "I'm sorry they treated you that way."

He frowns. "That's why I'm never going back. I signed a con-tract, and I'm sure if they find me, they can threaten me with enough lawsuits that I'll give in, so that's why I'm running. I don't want to be found. I don't want to be forced back into the spotlight."

Everything begins making perfect sense. "So if they get to close to finding you here . . ."

"Then I'll leave," he whispers. "Only now, being with you like this . . . it'll make it impossible for me to not look back."

Ace takes both of my hands in his. "I don't know exactly what this is, but it's real, and I'm tired of trying to fight it. I want you . . . and I want to see where this leads. If the reporters or my bitch of a tour manager, Jane Ann, get too close, I want you to leave with me."

I gasp. "I can't just leave this place behind . . . I have to stay and figure out how to get the taxes paid so everyone doesn't lose their homes."

"If the time comes, I'll pay for the taxes. You can leave Birdie or Adele in charge, and we'll leave—just you and me."

I debate what exactly I'm agreeing to here if I say yes—a life on the run like a fugitive. "I don't know if I can do that."

"It won't be forever, Iris. We'll come back eventually, after the frenzy surrounding the band and my disappearance dies down. What I need is a good attorney who can read my contract and give me some solid advice."

That doesn't sound so bad. His plan seems logical, and I completely understand his reasoning for not facing the label and the media until he's ready. But besides all that, I don't want to be without him. He's worth leaving everything behind for a while.

Finally, I nod. "Okay. I'll go with you when the time comes, but in the meantime you can talk to Mr. Stern. He's the attorney who handled Gran's estate, and I've known him my entire life. You can trust him."

Ace nods. "Okay, we'll have to go to Sarah's house in Columbus and get my contract so the attorney can go over it."

Ace grins and pulls me into him, suddenly seeming extremely happy. "Thank you."

"For what?" I ask, confused because I haven't really done anything to be thanked for.

"For agreeing to leave with me, and"—he gives me a wry smile—"for agreeing to be mine. No one has ever belonged to me before."

I raise my eyebrow, not believing that this sweet, intelligent, beautiful man before me has never had anyone be his before. "No one?"

He shakes his head. "No one has ever been the total package before—just you, Iris. You're the one."

This is all happening so fast, but I don't care. I'm not going to allow the logical side of my brain to ruin this happiness for me. For now I will revel in it. For now I am his.

Chapter 16

ACE

I readjust my arm and then trace my fingers along Iris's skin as she sleeps. Now that I'm allowed, I can't bring myself to stop touching her. I always feared that having the chance to share intimate moments like this with her would cause me to have an addiction, and I was right.

I sigh as I watch her in peaceful slumber. Yes, I'm afraid that it's far too late for me to back out of this now. She's already taken a piece of my heart, so I don't know at this point if it was ever possible to stop this from happening.

It's almost as if we were fated to be.

I place my lips softly against her forehead, and she stirs, moving slowly, stretching her muscles awake. "Good morning, beautiful."

She snuggles into my side and pulls the blanket up around her shoulders. "Good morning."

"Are you hungry?"

She nods and then giggles. "Yes, considering we skipped dinner last night and went straight for dessert . . . all night long."

A grin spreads across my face as I remember back to exactly how many ways we had our dessert last night. I don't think I'll ever get tired of hearing this stunning creature moan my name in moments of unadulterated bliss.

A little growl rumbles low in her belly and I laugh. "Yes. I will most definitely have to remember to feed you from here on in."

"If only we could live on the dessert alone, then we'd never have to leave this bed." She sighs happily.

"That'd be nice," I agree, and then her stomach rumbles again, causing me to sit up. "I'll be right back."

She frowns and touches my wrist. "Don't take too long."

I laugh and touch the tip of her nose with my index finger. She's adorable when she pouts.

I whip into the kitchen and grab the pizza box out of the fridge. I go to the cabinet Iris got the plates from last night and get a clean one and begin loading it down with as many slices as it will hold.

After heating the food up in the microwave, I grab a can of soda from the fridge and rush back into the bedroom.

I sit on the edge of the bed and set the plate between us. "Sustenance."

"Indeed." Iris smiles at me, her green eyes dancing with amusement, and I know there's something weighing on her mind. "Can I ask you something?"

I raise an eyebrow and eye her with mock suspicion. "I thought you said you Internet stalked me. What else could that inquisitive brain of yours want to know?"

She blushes. "I really am sorry about that. I just wanted to know you."

"It's okay, Iris, really. It's fine. I would've probably done same thing if I were in your shoes. You didn't know me from Adam, and I was acting like a crazy man—so hot and cold with you."

She sighs. "Still, it was wrong, but I'm glad we've got everything out in the open now."

"Me too," I agree. "So what is it that you want to ask me about?"

"Well . . ." she begins, but hesitates. "Last night—the tattoo about Shakespeare and the quotes—how do you know all that stuff? Most guys can't even name one classic play, let alone use Shakespearean quotes in just the right moments off the top of their heads."

I take a drink of soda and then pass her the can, from which she eagerly drinks. "It started when I was about thirteen or so, I guess. My foster mom was a huge reader. She loved the classics, and her favorite was Shakespeare. She always told me a man who could quote the lines from one of the most romantic men of all time could woo the heart of any woman. So, being the loner I was, and desperate to find a girl who would love me someday, I did like I always do—I studied. The crazy thing is, I ended up loving it. The written word is a beautiful thing. It's one of the things that initially inspired me to write songs."

"So did it work?" she asks with a shy smile, and I tilt my head, causing her to elaborate. "The quoting?"

I grin at her wickedly and raise my eyebrows suggestively. "You tell me. You're the only girl I've ever exposed that side of myself to."

"I am?" she asks timidly.

I nod. "No one has ever inspired me to say them . . . that is, not until you. You, I could write songs about all day."

She bites her bottom lip, and I love the look of adoration on her face as she stares at me. "I love that I inspire you. I hope I continue to do that."

I reach over and cup her cheek in the palm of my hand. "Just by being, you'll do that."

After we finish our breakfast of leftovers, I reluctantly kiss her good-bye so I can go back to my own trailer to shower and change my clothes. While eating our pizza, we made plans to drive to Columbus to Mom's house in order for me to retrieve my contract. Iris convinced me that Mr. Stern is a trustworthy man—one who is perfectly capable of letting me know what my options are.

I told Iris what it was like at Mom's funeral and how reporters seemed to be everywhere I turned, cornering me and not allowing me to grieve the loss of the only mother I'd ever really known. Instead, the reporting leeches were interested only in getting the scoop on why I had walked off stage and if I had any plans to return to fulfill the rest of my tour.

I don't understand why they even care. Honestly, I never got this much press before. Paparazzi were never an issue. I guess the world is just that intrigued by what would motivate a guy like me to walk away from everything he'd worked hard to get. Someone walking away from money and fame rarely ever happens.

When I make it back to Iris's place, she opens the door and wraps me immediately in a warm embrace. "I missed you."

I nuzzle into her neck and inhale the sweet floral scent of her body wash and perfume. "I've been gone less than an hour."

She sighs against me. "I know. I can't help it, though, I find you kind of addicting."

My heart beats faster, loving that my crazy obsession with her is, well, a mutual thing.

I pull back and ask, "You ready to head out?"

She nods. "Let me grab the keys to the car first. I figure it might hide you better than that bike."

My girl's so smart. "Good thinking."

She tosses me the keys and I catch them with ease. "You can drive. You know where we're going."

The drive to Columbus goes by rather quickly with Iris along for the ride. She brought along a few of her favorite CDs of musical soundtracks but can't manage to get them to play, so we opt to sing together. I surprise her by actually knowing a few of the lyrics to the songs she sings.

"Did you study theater too?" She laughs, still amazed by my knowledge of the subject.

I shake my head. "No, but I did join the choir in high school. I took any opportunity I could to sing. It didn't matter what it was, as long as it had soul behind the words, I loved it."

Her green eyes widen and she stares at me from the passenger seat of the car with her mouth agape.

After a moment of her just looking at me like I've grown another head, I can't help myself from asking, "What?"

She shakes her head like she's waking herself from a daze. "I can't tell you how many times I've said the very same thing. I actually drive Birdie nuts with my opinions of today's music. It lacks soul."

I smile, loving that we've found another thing we connect on. "That's exactly what my problem is with all the shit music I've been turning out to the world as Wicked White. The lyrics don't mean anything substantial. I hate that I don't get to lend more than just my voice to a song. They tell me how to sing—even what kind of emotion I need to feel when I sing it. The songs—they're just not me."

Iris furrows her brow, her green eyes fixed on me. "Can't you just demand to have input? I mean, it is your career."

I sigh as I adjust my hands on the wheel. "Believe me, I've tried. Jane Ann, my manager, is intractable when it comes to making changes that can affect her bottom line. Fans are eating the crap up that the band has been putting out, so she has denied me at every turn when I suggest any kind of change."

"I'm sorry, Ace. I can only imagine how tough that must've been for you."

I reach over and take her hand in mine and bring her knuckles up to my lips. "Thank you. But it doesn't matter anymore, seeing as how I never want to go back. Not to the way things were, anyhow."

When we pull into my old neighborhood on the east side of Columbus, I keep my eyes peeled for any cameras, but to my surprise when Sarah's old, white two-story comes into view, there's not a single soul on the street.

Hopefully I'm no longer the hot story and they've moved on.

I park out by the curb and cut the engine. There's a mountain of emotions building inside me as I sit here. On one hand I can't wait to show Iris where I grew up, but on the other hand I know I'll be gutted the moment I step through that door. When I buried Sarah, I couldn't bring myself to go inside. I stayed in the hotel and came by only to make sure the place was locked tight before I took off. I knew right after she died the wound to my heart was too fresh to handle coming into a house that reminds me so much of her, but I think with Iris by my side that I can handle it.

This isn't exactly the best neighborhood, but shockingly, the house appears to be untouched.

"Hey," Iris whispers softly and gives my hand a little squeeze. "You okay?"

It's then I realize I haven't said a word since I shut off the car, but simply sat here gazing at the house, building the courage to go inside.

I nod and give her a small smile. "I'm fine, just a little sad, I guess."

"I understand. At first, being at home without Gran, it was rough. In a weird way, throwing myself into going through her things made me feel closer to her. It reminded me of all the good times I shared with her. It's going to be hard when you first go in there, but I'm here for you, and I promise, it'll be okay."

I lean over and cup her face, bringing it to mine so I can kiss her lips. We both shut our eyes, trusting in one another, knowing we're here for each other even when it seems that we are lone souls in this world. It's nice to not feel so alone anymore.

"You're amazing, you know that?" I tell her.

She blushes. "I think you're pretty great too."

After a few more stolen kisses, I take a deep breath. "I think it's time we go inside before I end up taking you right here in the car. I'm sure the neighbors would enjoy the show, but, well, you know how I feel about sharing you."

Iris laughs and my heart warms. Her laughter is one of the best sounds in the world and is quickly becoming one of my favorite things.

"We better go then." She gives me a wry grin.

We walk hand in hand up the sidewalk. I fish out the keys, and when we step up onto the small concrete porch, I unlock the door.

Even though Sarah was only my foster mother, she treated me like I was her real flesh and blood. When I turned eighteen and she no longer got paid to keep me, she never once made a move to kick me out. Instead, she encouraged me to stay and go on to college once I graduated high school. Even when I did leave to attend Ohio State, she kept my bedroom exactly the same, like a real mother would do for her son. That's how I knew she really loved me. I mean, I thought she did prior to that because she showed it in every one of her actions toward me, but that proved it. Before her, I'd never lived with someone who wasn't always anxious to get rid of me.

I flip the lights on when we enter the small living room. Sarah always kept the curtains drawn shut, said the light affected the television and irritated her when she tried to watch her daytime soaps.

The rest of the house is just as she left it: magazines on the coffee table, her nearly empty coffee mug from what I'm sure was her fifth cup that day, and of course her small library filled with classic books next to her television.

Iris steps in and immediately focuses her attention on the small bookcase near the front door that houses all of Mom's favorite photos. "Is this you?"

I come up behind her and wrap my arms around her waist and rest my chin on her shoulder. My eyes zero in on the picture of me in junior high with slicked-back hair she's pointing to. "Yep, that's me."

She laughs. "Are you wearing a tuxedo in your school picture?"

I laugh as I recall the day clearly. "Yes. I was an usher in Mom's cousin's wedding and I fell in love with the tux. I was nearly fourteen and had never worn anything so fancy and didn't want to take it off, so Mom paid a couple extra days rental so I could have my school picture taken in it the following Monday after the wedding."

She leans back into me and I burrow my nose into her hair and inhale her scent again. That's becoming one of my most favorite scents.

"You were too cute," she says and then twists so she can gaze up at me. "Will you show me your room?"

I nod and pull on her hand to follow me. The old stairs creak under our feet as we climb to the second level. When we reach the top, I pull her down the hall to my old bedroom. Before I take her in, I yank her against me and back her into the closed door and crush my lips to hers, causing her to groan.

I pull back to gaze upon her face, trying to halt myself from becoming too excited.

She's grinning. "Are you always so anxious when you bring girls to your bedroom?"

I lean my forehead against hers. "I've never brought a girl here before. I just wanted to kiss you one last time before you go in and see my room."

She cocks her head. "Why?"

This time it's me who blushes. "I'm afraid when you go in there you might question my manliness."

She laughs and shimmies her hips against mine, and her grin widens as she feels my semierect cock pushing against her through my jeans. "Trust me. You're plenty man enough." Iris pauses for a beat and finds the knob behind her and twists. "Let's see what you're so afraid of me seeing."

Without another word she flings open the door and steps through its threshold backward. I hold my breath as she spins on her heel and takes in the sight of my sanctuary.

"Wow . . ." she says with a breathy voice. "You weren't kidding when you said you were a Shakespeare addict."

I lean against the doorjamb as she wanders into my room to inspect things more closely. All of my walls are exactly as I left them, covered in posters for plays William Shakespeare wrote. The nightstand beside my bed is still stacked with a pile of books, most of which matched Mom's collection downstairs. I think she bought me copies because she got tired of me borrowing hers all the time.

My eyes follow Iris as she stops at what I like to call my reward wall. Mom was so proud of me every time I got recognition of some kind. It was hard to talk her out of displaying them all and persuade her to put up only the most important ones, like my high school diploma, along with my valedictorian letter and my bachelor's degree from Ohio State.

"A degree in philosophy. Why doesn't that surprise me?" Iris turns to me and quirks an eyebrow. "You're kind of like a genius, huh?"

I laugh. "I don't know about a genius . . . well educated, yes."

She finishes inspecting my room and runs her fingers along my dresser before she flips through the stack of CDs sitting there. "How did you get into music?"

I walk over next to her and turn around to rest my hands behind me as I lean against the dresser. "Mom bought me an old guitar at a yard sale. I, of course, taught myself how to play and to read music, and while I'm definitely no Shakespeare, I've found I'm pretty good at writing lyrics."

She wraps her hands around my waist. "A self-taught man . . . I like it." Iris presses her lips to mine and then frowns. "So, after seeing all this . . . it doesn't explain how you were able to fight so well. A guy like you, book smart, isn't typically quick with his fists like you were with Jeremy that day."

I frown. "Unfortunately, when you're an unconventional man like me, it attracts the kinds of guys who like to assert their dominance over someone they perceive to be weak. It was unlucky for them that I knew how to fight. I wasn't the mousy little nerd they expected when they messed with me. I had no problem fighting back, because using my fists to protect myself was the only thing I'd ever known. Of course, that was before Mom showed me there was another way to live without fighting constantly. I think for the longest time all the counselors had it in my file that I was a kicker."

I chuckle at that last thought, but stop when Iris's beautiful lips turn down into a deep frown. I pull on the hem of her shirt. Her eyes begin to fill with tears, and I slide my finger under her chin and tip it up so I can gaze into her eyes. "Hey, don't be sad for me. I turned out okay."

A tear slips down her cheek. "I'm sorry you had to go through that. Was it horrible living with your real mother before you went into the foster system?"

I sigh. "It wasn't pleasant, but at the time I didn't know there was any other way to live, so I was unaware of exactly how bad it was. When the state came to take me away, I didn't want to go with them. I fought every counselor, every foster family, teacher . . . anyone who I thought at the time was keeping me from being with my real mom. It wasn't until Sarah came into my life that things got better and I wanted to change myself."

"I used to feel that way about my mom too. It wasn't until I found out she was dead that I really gave up hope of her ever wanting me back, because obviously, by then, that dream was dead just like she was. I can't imagine what my life would've been like if I didn't have Gran . . ." Iris shakes her head and then wraps her hands around my neck and twirls the hair at my nape around her fingers. "I'm glad you had Sarah. I would've loved to have met her."

I hug her tighter against my chest. "She would've loved you."

The mention of the word love causes her eyes to snap in my direction, and a strange intensity flows between us. It's crazy to even entertain the idea of loving Iris so soon, but I know deep down that this is exactly what I'm feeling. It's almost as if our story emulates some of the greatest love stories in history. The tales of two people who barely know one another, yet have such a strong connection that their passion is unfathomable to outsiders.

I just can't bring myself to tell Iris that this is what I'm feeling just yet. If she finds out I love her so intensely this soon, it may scare her off.

With a regretful sigh, I pull back a bit. "I think it's time we get that contract and head back before it starts to get late. It's too risky to stay here much longer. Camera crews could be anywhere, and we don't want to push our luck."

She reluctantly nods and drops her hands from around my neck, seemingly deflated that I didn't capitalize on the romantic moment we just shared. "You're right."

It kills me to disappoint her. I know we're already in this deep together, and it probably wouldn't totally shock her if I told her everything I'm feeling, but I just don't want to continue moving our relationship so fast for fear it'll stop at any moment.

IRIS

I t's been nearly a week since we were at Ace's childhood home, and I swear we shared a moment when we were wrapped up in one another's arms in his bedroom. I nearly told him I loved him in that moment, but thought better of it immediately because I don't want him thinking I'm saying that merely because I know who he is. When I tell him that I love him, I want him to know that I mean it with each inch of my beating heart.

I stare up at his face while his chest rises and falls in a rhythmic pattern as he sleeps soundly next to me in my bed. His face is stunning with his chiseled, strong jawline and full lips that seem to have a resting pout to them even when he's relaxed, and his prominent nose completes the features any male model would be envious of. His crazy, wild hair is even sexy when he sleeps. I'm constantly tempted to slide it through my fingers.

Ever since the first night we made love, we've spent every night together—each night being even more magical than the last, making me fall for him a little more. I've been saying a little prayer every night that he's never found and can stay here with me just like this forever, but deep down I know that's not reality, and it scares the shit out of me.

I don't want him to leave, and the thought of me leaving with him—it excites and terrifies me at the same time. I'm not sure if I'm cut out for a life on the run, and more importantly, I'm not ready to give up on my dreams that have already been put on hold. I'll have to return to New York at some point—with or without Ace.

I refuse to be that girl who gets so swept up in a man that she tosses everything aside for him, losing her dreams and identity. That's not me.

Ace stirs below me, and I know he's in the process of waking.

I place a soft kiss on his lips as our naked bodies remain pressed together. "Good morning. Hungry?"

"Starving," he whispers and pulls my face back up to his, letting me know that he's not just talking about food here.

He shifts and pulls me on top of him, where he cups my ass as he deepens our kiss.

This man is insatiable.

I bring my legs down around his hips and press my knees into the mattress below us, careful to keep his stiff cock outside of my body.

He moans when I rotate my hips a couple times, sliding him against my slick folds and enjoying the feel of his skin against my most sensitive body part.

"God . . . Iris," he growls.

I love when I make the normally collected Ace go a little caveman. It seems that I have this ability to make him lose his control . . . and I like that . . . a lot.

The calluses from playing the guitar make his hands a little rough, but I love the way they feel sliding up the bare skin of my back when he's enjoying my body.

The friction of the tip of him hitting my clit over and over causes me to moan this time and then whisper, "I need you."

He turns to my nightstand and grabs the box of condoms. A frown immediately etches into his perfect features, and I stop writhing against him, sitting up. "Are we out?"

Ace's lips pull into a tight line. "Yeah. We went through that box really fast. I planned on getting more today because I knew we were getting low."

I sigh, deflated, but still completely turned on, and I know he is as well because his hard length is still pressing into me. "I'm on birth control . . . and we are exclusive . . . right?"

I allow my thought to trail off, not wanting to seem so forward with my request.

Ace traces my lips with his long fingers. "Are you sure . . . ? We don't have to. I can wait."

I kiss his fingers and nod. "I'm yours, right? And you're mine?"

"Irrevocably, on both accounts," he answers. "But I want you to be sure. I don't want you to make a rash decision because you're horny."

I smile down at him. "If we belong to one another, I don't see how this would be a rash decision."

He's quiet for a beat, and knowing now how intelligent Ace is, I'm sure he's contemplating every scenario before giving in to me. "You're right, but I want you to know that I've never done this before. You'll be my first. Have you . . . ?"

I shake my head. "Never. I always made Tanner use protection. I guess I never trusted him." I peer into his eyes as a revelation occurs to me. "But I trust you, implicitly."

Ace licks his lips like he's suddenly nervous. "So you've only ever been with Tanner?"

"Yes," I answer honestly, and my face reddens at the admission that I've only ever been with one man in my twenty-two years.

But that's got me curious, and I can't help myself from asking the question that nags at every woman when she thinks about her man and his sexual history. "How many people have you been with?"

His eyes drift away from my face, and my heart drops, knowing more than likely that means it's going to be a number that I don't want to hear from a man whose unprotected penis I'm about to let inside me.

"Ace . . . ?" Even I can hear the worry in my voice while I await his answer.

His gaze flicks back to mine. "It's hopefully not as bad as you're thinking, but it's a number that I'm not proud of . . . it's a number that happened before I made a commitment to myself that I was worth loving and that someday I would find a woman who loved me."

I swallow hard. "Do I really want to know? Is it that bad?"

He shrugs. "The feeling that emulated love was something I was addicted to for a while. I found it easily in the arms of random women who wanted to use me for sex. Psychologists would probably say I used women to fill the void I felt when my mother gave me away. And in a weird way, I'm sure that's partly true, but I know that I was smart enough to figure out that *that* wasn't love I was feeling. It was a way to temporarily forget that I was once unloved and so easily discarded. So, once I figured that out in my early twenties, after attending a few psych classes, I stopped randomly fooling around."

I furrow my brow. "So before me . . . ?"

"I haven't had sex in a while," he admits. "Sure, there were times I slipped back into my old ways, but for the most part I've been pretty good at abstaining."

My mouth drops open. I'm completely floored by this news, and honestly, I can't wrap my head around it. "You mean you don't sleep with random groupies on a daily basis?"

Ace shakes his head. "No. Not even close."

"Wow . . . I thought all rock stars slept with their groupies every chance they got."

He gives me a half smile. "Not all of us."

"Apparently," I tease. "The association of rock stars may revoke your membership card if this ever gets out."

"I don't care." He laughs. "Let them. I'm through with that life, anyhow. I've got all I need being here with you. I could give a shit about the music industry at this point. I'll get a job somewhere, anywhere you want to live, and I'll use my musical talents to serenade you."

I lean down and press my lips to his. "I could get used to being serenaded. You're going to spoil me and ruin me for all other men. No one will ever be able to live up to you."

Ace grins. "Good, I don't want any other man to have a chance in hell. Besides, I don't plan on ever leaving you."

Warmth floods my heart. Hearing him say that he's never going to leave me is the sweetest sound I've ever heard. It makes me crave him that much more.

"Make love to me," I whisper. "I want to be yours in every possible way."

That's all the permission he needs and he rolls me over, pressing his weight on top of me. His hand slides over the mound of my breast, over my collarbone and against my neck until his thick fingers thread into my hair. Kisses from his sensual lips follow, setting my skin on fire as he finds his way to my mouth.

When his tongue darts out and traces the entrance of my mouth, I open, giving him full access. I spread my legs wider, squirming below him with anticipation, needing to feel him inside of me, moving with nothing between us.

With one swift movement, Ace buries himself deep inside me. His eyes burn with fiery passion as he pulls back and then rocks into me again.

He groans as he leans down next to my ear and whispers, "Jesus. I can't believe you're mine."

A shudder rips through me as I close my eyes and revel in the pure romanticism in his voice. Those words—those sweet, sweet words wrapping around my heart, making me feel so loved and so wanted—are nearly enough to make me admit to Ace just how I feel about him.

Strong arms slip under me and wrap around my shoulders as he continues his deliciously slow, rhythmic pace. Each thrust causes my core to burn with even more need for this man.

I reach behind him and grab his muscular ass in my hands, loving the way each muscle moves as he continues to please me. "Oh, Ace. That's it."

He rises up, still working himself into me. "Don't come yet. The sounds you make will send me over the edge, and I'm nowhere near done with you. I want to make this last. You feel . . . God, Iris. You feel fucking amazing." He leans down and whispers against my mouth, "It's like your body was made just for me."

A tremble rushes through me, and I know he asked me to wait, but there's no way of stopping the impending orgasm that's about to spread through me.

I dig my nails into his backside. "Oh, God. Ace. I'm coming. I can't stop . . . ohhhh."

His rhythm picks up speed, and he pounds into me much harder and much faster than he was before, intensifying my pleasure before his movements go rigid and he closes his eyes and growls as he comes hard inside me.

When he opens his eyes and simply gazes at me with a look that can only be explained as pure awe, like I'm the most amazing thing he's ever seen, I can no longer fight it. I know without a shadow of a doubt that I'm wholeheartedly in love with Ace Johnson, but I'm scared to tell him.

Later that afternoon, when Ace and I can find the strength to pull ourselves away from my bed, I walk him to the door while he pulls his shirt over his head.

When I open the front door for him, he pulls me into his tight embrace and kisses me. "Would it be weird if I say I miss you every minute that we're not together?"

I laugh and shake my head. "No, because I feel exactly the same way." I giggle as he kisses my neck, but then playfully push him back. "Go shower before I change my mind and drag you back to my room."

He waggles his eyebrows. "That's definitely not a threat."

I push him back once more and laugh. "Go."

As Ace heads down my front steps, he buttons and zips his jeans. My face instantly reddens when I notice Tanner's car parked in front of my place, knowing he's seen us and the way Ace is still practically getting dressed while walking out my front door.

Ace passes by the car just as Tanner opens the driver's door and gets out. He gives Ace a curt nod, and Ace instantly stops in his tracks and whips back around to stare at me with an expression that clearly asks if I need him to stay.

I shake my head, and he pulls his lips into a tight line as if he doesn't like my answer, but he obliges by heading around the corner to his own place.

Tanner pulls a pair of dark sunglasses off his face as he approaches me. He's not in a suit today, but in a more relaxed outfit of jeans and a light blue button-down. The dark hair on his head is styled back, making the cool blue tone of his eyes stand out more.

He's attractive, but he's a sleazy asshole.

Tanner glances back in the direction Ace just went and then raises one eyebrow as he turns back to stare up at me. "I guess you weren't kidding when you said you've moved on."

I fold my arms over my chest and suddenly regret not throwing a bra on as I dressed in a tank top and pair of shorts to walk Ace out. "What do you want, Tanner?"

He sighs as he rests his hand on the wooden railing of my porch. "Can't I come in?"

I shake my head. "No. We can talk just fine out here."

His shoulders slump a bit. Guys like Tanner Lawrence aren't used to hearing the word no too often. "I wanted to stop by and let you know that I explained your situation to my higher-ups and was able to get you a thirty-day extension, which means you have two months from now to get the money together to pay the taxes before the state moves forward with seizing the trailer park. It was the best I could do."

"Why would you do that?" I ask, but I'm grateful that he did. I've been here only a month and I never had any intention of staying long-term. I wanted to get back to my life in New York as soon as I could, but this extension changes a situation that I thought was impossible to fix to one I might have a long shot at fixing if I get a job quickly. I was nearly ready to give up on Willow Acres since there was no way I could come up with twenty thousand dollars in thirty days.

Besides, my relationship with Ace changes things too. I won't run back to New York immediately like I planned . . . at least not until Ace figures out what he's going to do. By sticking around here a little longer, I might have a real shot at saving my home.

I pull myself out of my thoughts to stare down at Tanner. "Thank you, Tanner. I really appreciate that."

Tanner gives me a sad smile, making one of his dimples stand out prominently. "It was no trouble at all. I'd like to believe we're still friends. I know I did you wrong, and you've got every right to hate me, so I figured using what little bit of power I have to help you is the least I can do. I'm sorry I was such an asshole while we were together, Iris."

For the first time since we broke up nearly two years ago, I finally believe Tanner's apology. But it's not enough to erase the hurt and humiliation he caused me, so the second chance he's begged me for over the last couple years still isn't going to happen.

I sigh as I stare down at him and smile. "I forgive you, but this doesn't change anything between us. It's still over."

He picks at a knot in the handrail. "Who was the guy, anyway? I haven't seen him around here before."

I stiffen, not wanting to answer any questions about who Ace is. "He's new in town."

"That's what I figured. Where's he from and what's he doing here? It's not like there are jobs around here or anything. No one chooses to just up and move to Sarahsville."

After a second of quick thinking, I make up the very first thing that pops into mind to help throw him off wanting to find out anything else about Ace. "He was Sadie Hill's nephew. He moved into her old place since he was one of the heirs in her will."

Tanner narrows his blue eyes at the trailer next to mine. "I didn't know Sadie had any family. I always thought it was just her." He turns back to me. "Well, be careful. You don't know him, and I would hate to have to beat the shit out of him for hurting you."

I open my mouth to say thanks again, but is that really something I want to thank him for? Instead, I give him a half smile. "Thanks for the tax extension, Tanner. I'll try my hardest to get enough money to you by the end of the sixty days."

He nods. "Okay. I'll see you around, Iris. Call me if you need me." His eyes flick to Ace's place, then back to me. "I mean it, anything you need, get in touch with me."

After Tanner leaves, I hurry into the shower. A brilliant idea occurs to me and I can't wait to get it set in motion. I dry off and then rush into the kitchen and dial Birdie's work number.

"Angel's," a rough man's voice answers after two rings.

"Hi. May I speak with Birdie, please? It's Iris," I reply.

"Hold on." There's a distinct sound of the receiver hitting the counter before the man yells across the room, "Birdie, phone's for you."

"Who is it?" I hear my friend ask from a distance, making her voice barely audible.

"That hot friend of yours that you had in here the other night, Flower or something," the guy replies, and I roll my eyes at his description of me.

"You mean Iris, dickwad." Birdie's voice is so much closer now, like she's coming to it, and then she picks up the phone. "What's up, girlie?"

"Hey. Sorry to bother you at work, but I wanted to ask you if Angel was hiring?"

"Um, not sure. I know we had a girl quit last week because she's pregnant and starting to show. Her tips were for shit. The asshole male species apparently have some moral code about flirting with a pregnant chick and always asked to be seated in a different section, giving her no choice but to quit. So yeah, we might. Let me ask." She lowers the phone. "Angel, you filled Megan's spot yet? You know you'll need the extra help once I start second shift later this week."

The same guy who answered the phone mumbles something about the size of my chest, and I raise my eyebrows, thinking of how he just called me hot moments ago. I didn't know Angel himself was so crude.

I hear the two of them talking back and forth, but her hand must be over the phone because I can barely make out what they're saying.

"You're hired!" Birdie says into the phone, and I can feel the excitement in her voice. "Be ready at nine in the morning, I'll pick you up and train you tomorrow."

"Wow," I say, completely flabbergasted at how easy that was. "Thank you so much, Birdie. I owe you one."

She laughs. "Big-time. I'll see you after I get off tonight. I haven't seen you much lately, and we need to totally catch up."

"Sounds good. See you then." I hang up after telling her goodbye and am hopeful that I'll be able to gather enough money if I save every penny I can to keep this place without becoming Ace's charity case. I don't want him to think I'm using him for money.

When Birdie walks in my door later that evening, she stops dead in her tracks the moment she spots Ace and me cozied up on the couch together. Her eyes widen and then she gives me a sly grin. "Is he the reason you've been MIA on me all week?"

I bite my lip and blush as I flick my line of sight from Birdie to Ace and then back. I shrug a little. "Yes."

As if that's his cue, Ace leans over and kisses my cheek. "I'll let you guys have some time."

I turn and kiss his lips. "I'll come over in a bit."

He smiles and then pushes himself up off the couch and heads out the door.

As soon as the door shuts behind Ace, Birdie folds her arms across her chest and gives me a pointed look—a look she gives whenever she's pissed that someone's been holding out on her.

I hold my hands up defensively. "I was going to tell you."

She quirks an eyebrow. "When? After you ran off with him and had a bunch of adorable little mini-Aces?"

I twist my lips. "I deserve that. You're my best friend. I should've told you."

"You're damn straight, because what if he kidnapped you or something and I had no information to give the cops. What kind of best friend would that make me?"

"A fantastic one?" I say with a hopeful voice, trying to dig myself out of a hole, but it doesn't seem to be working with her, so I shove myself off the couch and hold my arms out. "I'm sorry. Can we hug it out if I promise to fill you in now?"

She tries hard to force a scowl, but eventually it turns into a smile and she rolls her eyes before stepping into my embrace. "Okay, tell me everything, and don't leave out any of the juiciness."

I laugh and pull her down on the couch with me and tell her everything I can about Ace and our time together, only leaving out the part where he's the missing rock star everyone is going gaga over trying to find. That would totally warp her mind.

It's not that I don't trust Birdie with Ace's secret, because I totally would—I'd trust her with my own life—but the truth is, it's not my secret to tell. I hope if the truth comes out, she can respect that.

When I finish telling her everything, Birdie turns toward me and props her head up against her arm that is resting against the back of the couch. "Wow. Shakespeare? Really? Him? I would've never pictured that."

I nod and giggle. "He's a true romantic."

She bites her lip, and I know from the expression on her face that something's weighing on her mind.

"Okay, out with it," I say.

Birdie sighs and flips her blond hair over her shoulder. "I don't want you to think that I'm not happy for you, because I totally am. I mean, he sounds perfect, and I can tell you're really falling for the guy."

"But . . ." I prod, sensing the hesitation in her voice.

"*But*, we still don't know much about him, and that scares me for you. I know how sensitive you are when it comes to your heart. You're an all-or-nothing girl, Iris. When you love, you love hard and deep. I just hope he's as serious about you as you are about him."

I want to argue with her—tell her that she's wrong and that she has absolutely nothing to worry about because I know Ace. I know he's got a good heart and his intentions with me are pure, but when I see the concern in Birdie's eyes, it just makes me love her that much more.

I wrap my arms around her and squeeze her tight. "I'll be careful. I promise."

It's an easy promise to make because I know deep down that I don't have anything to worry about.

Right on schedule, Birdie's at my house bright and early the next day to keep me on time for my first day on the job.

"Here." She tosses me a T-shirt as soon as she steps through my door. "Angel will give you a few of your own, so just return it to me when he does."

I stare down at a bright red shirt that's identical to the one Birdie's wearing, with the words "Angel's Girl" stretched across her chest, before yanking the shirt I have on off and replacing it with this too-small shirt. "Are all the shirts supposed to be this tight?"

My best friend laughs as she double-checks the lipstick she's applying in the reflection of the gold cap of the tube. "They are if you want good tips." Her eyes roam over me, appraising my outfit. "You look good. You might even make tips on your very first day."

It's going to be hard for me to gain enough courage to use my body as a tip magnet like Birdie does. She's got the body for it. She's voluptuous, while my appeal is more athletic. I never had to flaunt myself at any of the waitressing jobs I've had before.

On the way to Cambridge, Birdie does an excellent job of filling me in on all the workplace drama that I'm about to walk into, telling me who to make friends with and who to avoid. She runs down the list of pointers, and I suddenly wish I had brought a notepad to write them all down on. I'll never remember everything she's telling me.

Birdie hasn't worked at Angel's long, but she's managed to use her looks, wit, and good work ethic to move pretty high up on Angel's favorite waitresses list. She thinks I will do the same and we'll eventually work the night shift together, where all the real tip money is to be made.

A few hours into the job, I'm handling tables on my own like I'd been there for years. Having a ton of waitressing experience helped me pick things up quickly. It'll take me awhile to learn everything on the menu as well as my way around the kitchen, but soon I hope to have all that mastered.

Birdie nudges my hip with hers as she steps up to the bar. "How's it going?"

I smile at her. "It's going great! Thank you so much for getting me this job. I need to make money any way I can to get the taxes paid since Tanner got me an extension to save Willow Acres. Everyone's depending on me."

She frowns. "I know, and that's totally not fair, but I respect the hell out of you for taking on the responsibility."

The rest of the day goes on pretty much the same, and I become a little more confident, which helps me breeze through my first day. When Birdie drops me off at home, I pull the money out of my pocket and lay it on the kitchen table so that I can count my tips.

It's not much, but I've managed to make sixty bucks on my very first day. If I can somehow manage to bring in one hundred dollars a day, and everyone in the park pays their rent on time for the next two months, I might have a shot at coming up with enough to pacify the state. Hopefully if I can give them half the money, they'll give me another extension to come up with the rest because they'll see how much I'm trying.

I guess only time will tell if I'll make it there or not.

ACE

Iris and I make the quick drive to the small town center of Sarahsville for an appointment with her grandmother's attorney. I'm glad Iris has the day off to come with me. I don't get to spend every waking minute with her anymore since she's gotten a job. It's amazing how lonely the trailer park can be now that I have to find things to fill my days.

I've busied myself doing odd jobs for the elderly residents around me. Earlier today I repaired a window that had been broken in Adele's trailer for the better part of six years. In exchange, Adele made me a home-cooked meatloaf for lunch.

I miss Iris like crazy when she's gone, but I respect her like crazy for working hard to save her childhood home, and I'm glad I've been able to be helpful to the people she cares about.

Iris points out the attorney's office, an old blue two-story house set in a historic-looking neighborhood. It's just down the street from the small grocery store I first stopped at when I got into town. I've been waiting all week for Mr. Stern to have time to sit down with me to go over my contract, and I'm hoping he has some good news for me.

When I put the car in park, Iris says, "I have to warn you about Mr. Stern's secretary. You lucked out when she wasn't here when we dropped the contract off."

I lift an eyebrow. "Okay . . ."

"She's a talker. The less said, the easier it'll be for you to get away."

I chuckle. "So be polite, but don't talk much. Got it. Anything else?"

"Nope." Iris smiles, and I can't resist leaning in and stealing a small kiss before we get out of the car.

The moment we walk into the old house that's been turned into an office, the secretary with a long, brown braid smiles at us. The front of her hair is teased sky-high like we're about to shoot a retro eighties rock video, and I fight the urge to raise my eyebrows at her appearance. "There you two are. I was looking forward to seeing you again, Iris."

"Hi, Melody," Iris says and then politely asks, "Is Mr. Stern ready to see us?"

Melody's lips are covered in a shade of orange and they make an *O* shape as she leans back in her chair while peering into the next room through the open door. "Bill? You ready for Mr. White?"

"It's Johnson, actually," I correct her.

Melody stares up at me and winks. "Right. I forgot." She returns to her leaning position and glances back into the room before returning her gaze to me. "Go on in."

"Thank you." I place my hand on the small of Iris's back and usher her into the room where Mr. Stern sits at his desk, waiting for us.

We're met with a pair of kind gray eyes beneath a set of bushy white eyebrows as unruly as the gray hair on his head. The suit he's got on looks vintage, but I'm sure it's the same style he's been wearing for the better part of fifty years and he's not trying to go retro. Like most people around here, Mr. Stern has some age on him, I'm guessing close to seventy years, and seems as nice as they come.

There's no computer on his desk, but every inch of it is covered with stacks and stacks of files and loose paperwork. The man is definitely old-school.

He stands, giving Iris a friendly hug before giving my hand a nice firm handshake. "How are you, young man?"

"Fine, sir. Yourself?"

He eases back down in his seat and gestures for us to sit in the brown chairs in front of his desk. "Oh, can't complain too much." He sighs. "Let's get on down to it, shall we?" Mr. Stern grabs a file out of one of the stacks to his left and lays it in front of him. "I've had a chance to read over the contract you brought in, and while I must say that I don't have a lot of experience dealing with matters such as yours, I am well versed in reading legally binding documents."

"Did you find anything in there that will help me?" I ask eagerly.

He frowns. "I didn't find anything other than a debilitating injury or death clause that will release you from your contract, so I'm afraid unless you want to fight a huge company like Mopar Records, you'll have to fulfill your contract—completing three full albums with them and the tours that have been scheduled."

My shoulders slump. This was exactly what I feared. "That's not good news."

"However, I did find a loophole that may satisfy your biggest complaint with the record label."

My hope rises again. "What is it?"

"I remembered how you said you were unhappy with your contract because you weren't able to have creative control over your brand and the song choices . . . well, there's a part in the contract that says you are able to exercise artistic rights to help enhance your brand, meaning if you feel something portrays you in a light that you don't want to be in, you can refuse."

"Like song choices for the new album?" I grab Iris's hand and squeeze excitedly.

He nods slowly. "Yes, but you'll still be required to do shows, and ultimately you'll still have to perform the songs that you hate right now until you produce more new material. But remember, just because you refuse to go along with their ideas, it doesn't mean that they have to accept your new vision for your brand either."

"That's fantastic news!"

Mr. Stern holds up his hand to cut off my excitement. "You're not out of the woods yet. You said you've not shown for how many shows now?"

I frown as I try to recall how many concerts I've missed since being here two months. "Counting the one I walked out on . . . seven, I think."

He grimaces. "They can still sue you over that, and I'm afraid that suit can go into the millions, based on what I imagine a tour like yours to be worth."

"Shit," I mutter. "So it's possible that they can take back everything I've earned up until this point."

"And then some," he adds.

"So, I still can't go back—not now. I can't afford it."

"Son," Mr. Stern says, "if you don't go back, you could make things worse for yourself. We can protest that you had a mental breakdown over the loss of your foster mother and you snapped. Any judge may take that into consideration and . . ."

"No," I say. "I won't use my foster mother for an excuse for something I did. I refuse to do that."

He sighs. "Well, I'm afraid it could be rough on you once they do catch up to you."

I stand, hearing enough, and stick out my hand. "Thank you for the advice. I appreciate it, but I'll take that contract back now."

He hands it to me and Iris stands by my side. "Be careful and don't do anything rash. If you need me again, you know where to find me."

I nod curtly before stepping out of his office and paying Melody for the consultation, blocking her incessant chatter out with the thoughts of me and Iris preparing to leave if need be.

Both Iris and I are quiet on the ride back to Willow Acres. I appreciate the time to allow my mind to ponder the best next move.

I have a million different reasons to hop on my bike and ride away into oblivion and only one reason to stay put. That one reason outranks everything else and is sitting right beside me, holding my hand as I drive her home. I can't bear the thought of being without her. Thinking about it now makes my stomach turn, and I take a deep breath to calm my nerves.

When I park the car outside of her trailer, she sighs longingly as she looks around.

She's not saying it, but I can sense the looming fear in her about the impending day when I'll have to abruptly leave. I just pray she sticks with what she promised me and is ready to leave too when that time comes.

I'm tempted to ask her right now if she's having second thoughts but think better of it, because if she is, I don't want to know. It will break my heart and I'm not ready to let her go just yet.

She opens her door and pauses to look over at me. "You spending the night?"

I nod. "If you want me to."

She peers up at me with her green eyes through thick lashes. "I'll always want you." She reaches over and squeezes my hand with her smaller one. "Always."

Later that night, after we've made love to the point that we're both near exhaustion, I grab the book I brought back from my old bedroom and flip it open to my favorite play by Shakespeare, *Romeo and Juliet*. I've been reading Iris to sleep nearly every night this week, and she seems to really enjoy it.

I love the gentle little sighs she makes when I read her a particularly romantic line.

I lick my lips and continue to read, "'But, soft! What light through yonder window breaks? It is the east, and Juliet is the sun! Arise, fair sun, and kill the envious moon, who is already sick and pale with grief that thou her maid art far more fair than she.'"

By act 4 Iris is sound asleep and I find myself absently stroking her soft hair as I continue to read on to *Hamlet*. About an hour into her sleep, she grows restless, tossing her head side to side and whimpering a bit.

I'm tempted to wake her in order to save her from the nightmare she's obviously having but freeze instantly when she whispers my name.

"Don't go, Ace. Don't leave me . . . I love you." Her words are just a little louder than a faint whisper, but they're as clear as day.

My heart swells at her unknowing admission to me, and more than anything I want to squeeze her against me and tell her just how much I love her in return, but I dare not wake my sleeping angel. Knowing that she loves me has given me the courage to finally tell her how deep my feelings run for her.

Tomorrow will be the start of our forever.

CELEBRITY POP BUZZ NIGHTLY

The camera zooms in on Linda Bronson, standing outside of an old, white two-story house. "Good evening, I'm Linda Bronson, and I'm coming to you live from Columbus, Ohio, just outside of the foster home that the missing rock star Ace White grew up in. After the passing of his foster mother, Sarah Johnson, this house as well as all the contents inside have been left to Ace in her will. There has been no reported activity inside the home since Ms. Johnson passed nearly three months ago until recently. Neighbors reported seeing a man fitting the approximate age of Ace White exit the home and enter an older-model Chevy Cavalier that was parked outside.

"The neighbors reported that the man they saw had short hair and no beard and was accompanied by a young woman with long, brown hair. While it's not confirmed, it is possible that the man was

Ace White, since there appears to be no forced entry into the home and nothing appears to be vandalized, according to police.

"Once again, Ace White's missing persons case is still open. His tour manager, Jane Ann Rogers, has raised the reward to fifty thousand dollars for information leading to the discovery of his whereabouts. For *Celebrity Pop Buzz Nightly*, I'm Linda Bronson."

IRIS

Practicing in the shed with Ace is much easier this time than the last time we were out here. The last time there was so much sexual tension flowing between us that I could barely concentrate on actually singing. All I wanted to focus on was the fact that he was so close—touching me—where I could smell the spicy, delicious scent on his skin.

Now that I get to have him any way I want him, being so close is much easier.

"Look me in the eye and project," Ace says as he stands in the far corner of the shed, watching me perform a number from *Guys and Dolls*. "If you want the audience to feel it, then you have to feel it and sing it loud enough for the people clear in the back to hear you. Give them no choice but to be wrapped up in your emotions with you."

I take a deep breath and count the beats and come into the song right on time, fixing my gaze on Ace. I belt the song out, believing each word that flows from my lips, hoping that it comes through as authentic.

Ace gives me a dazzling smile. "Yes. Give me more."

I smile, loving his praise, and the cheer in my voice comes through perfectly into a happy portion of the song. This only seems to please him more, so I continue reaching down deep to drag the emotion out and allow confidence to ring through my voice until the very last verse of the song.

When the final note plays, Ace claps his hands slowly. "Iris, that was amazing. When you go back to Broadway, they'll have no choice but to pick you for a role."

"Really?" I practically squeal. "You really think that'll happen?"

He steps up to me and wraps me in his strong, comforting embrace. "I do, because if you sing for them the way you do for me, they'll be blinded by the light coming from you. It will have them stepping all over themselves to have you in one of their productions."

I sigh. "That would be a dream come true."

"Just promise that when you become a big Broadway star someday you won't forget who you are and will stay true to the girl who's singing her heart out in this shed, who has a true passion for the music itself."

I reach up to his nape and curl a lock of his hair around my finger. "I promise."

Ace stares down at me for a long moment, unmoving and not saying a word, just remains there, taking me in. There's an odd expression in his eyes, and it has me curious as to what's going on inside that beautiful mind of his.

"What is it?" I ask.

He smiles shyly. "You said something last night that's gotten me thinking."

I tilt my head. "Oh?"

"You said . . ." He pauses for a beat. "You said that you loved me while you were asleep. At first I thought you were having a nightmare because you were so restless, but then you said my name, followed by saying that you love me."

Heat floods my cheeks. While I don't deny that's how I feel about him, because I very much do, it's hard to hear that I've admitted my innermost feelings to him while I was in a state of unconsciousness.

He slides his index finger under my jaw and then pinches my chin gently between his thumb and forefinger, forcing me to stare into his russet eyes. "Don't be embarrassed. I'm glad you said it. You can't control what truths your brain releases when you're asleep, so I know you meant it. And you have no idea how happy that makes me, because I've been thinking it for so long now, but I was afraid to say it, unsure if it was too soon to feel so deeply for you. I worried I might scare you away."

My heart flutters. Knowing he feels the same way makes me so giddy that I could do a backflip. He loves me, and I love him—this is exactly what I've been hoping for.

He swallows deeply. "I love you, Iris—with every inch of my soul, with every inch of my entire being. You . . ." He brings both hands up and pulls my face so close to his that I can feel the heat of his breath on my lips. "*You* are my Juliet."

I melt into his hands. "I love you too, Ace, so very much."

Ace leans forward and presses his lips to mine. "'My bounty is as boundless as the sea. My love as deep. The more I give to thee, the more I have, for both are infinite.'"

I grin. "We're meant to be just like all the star-crossed lovers you read about."

His thumbs rub the skin on my flushed cheeks. "I couldn't agree more. Only we won't end tragically, because we'll find a way to make this work."

Lying there, wrapped in Ace's arms, I sigh contentedly. My mind drifts to all the lyrics to love songs where people sing about chucking it all just to be with the person they love, and I find myself agreeing with them. I never imagined loving someone could feel like this—that it could make me feel so complete. I can't think of anything that I've ever wanted more than this.

In this moment, our love feels never ending.

Ace strokes the hair on my head, and it's so relaxing I close my eyes and simply enjoy his touch.

"Iris?" Ace's voice breaks through the silence that fills the room.

"Hmm." I turn and place my hand on his bare chest and then rest my chin on top of it so I can look him in the eye.

"I think, after hearing what Mr. Stern said, I should go face the record label."

My eyes widen, and the sleepiness I felt moments ago goes away as this sudden change of heart from him shocks me. After seeing his reaction to what the lawyer said, I thought going back was the last thing Ace would ever do. "Why? I mean what's changed?"

His chest rises as he takes in a deep breath and then pushes it out through his nose. "You. You've changed everything for me."

"Me?" I ask, completely confused. "What does being with me have to do with your music career?"

"Nothing and yet everything." He traces absentminded circles on my shoulder. "I want to be with you. I don't want to have to hide. I want our life together to be easy and uncomplicated. If I continue to run, it'll put stress on our relationship at some point. I don't want you to resent me for taking you away from everything. So, I think once I talk to Mr. Stern again to find out just how deep in shit I am, I'm going to make plans to go back to California for a while to get everything sorted out. Once the spotlight dies down and I get shit settled, I'll come back for you."

I shake my head. "I don't like that plan. It involves us being apart. I want to come with you."

"I know, baby, but you've got a life here, taking care of all the people here. Let's not forget you've got Broadway waiting on you. I don't want you being with me to affect you in any way, including your possible career. Once you go back and try to make it in show business, some directors will cast you simply because of your relationship with me, while others will shun you for the exact same reason."

I grimace. "Do you really believe that's what would happen?"

He nods. "The entertainment industry is a fickle business. Everyone involved in it is out to make a buck, and if they believe they can make cash off of controversy surrounding you, they'll cast you simply for that. No one is really your friend. No matter how much they lie to you and tell you that they are. If you weren't so damn talented and if it wasn't your dream, I would discourage you wholeheartedly from even entertaining the idea of going into show business. But I won't, because I know how much this means to you, and I'd be a dick not to cheer you on and give you the best possible shot at realizing your dream. So, trust me when I say keeping it secret that we're together is best for now."

I sigh, hating the idea of not being with him, but his reasoning makes sense. I would hate to cause problems for my career before it even starts. As much as I would love to argue and come up with a snappy comeback proving his theory wrong, I know tabloid gossip and the Internet can wreak all kinds of havoc on a person's life. It wouldn't be farfetched to entertain the idea that it would do the same to someone like me.

"How long do you think it will take for you to take care of everything?"

He shrugs. "I'm not sure."

I frown, not liking that he can't give me some idea about a timeline. "What am I supposed to do without you while you're out in California getting things straightened out?"

"What were your plans before you met me?" Ace asks.

I furrow my brow. "Before you, I had plans to wrap things with Gran's estate, leave Adele in charge, and get back to New York as quick as possible. Broadway is my dream, and I still want that . . ." I hesitate. "But I want you more."

He gives me a sad smile. "You shouldn't stop going after your dream because I'm in the picture. I don't ever want to hold you back, and we'll be back together before you know it."

I shake my head. "I don't like this. I don't like us being apart."

Ace sighs. "I won't make any rash decisions. I'll stay here with you until we get the tax situation fixed, and then when you go back to New York, I'll go back to California. After I get everything worked out, I'll come to you. We'll live together in New York."

I smile, liking that idea much more. "That's a plan I think I can live with, as long as you promise to hurry back to me as soon as you can."

He kisses the top of my head. "I don't think I could stay away from you any longer than I ever had to."

Satisfied with his answer, knowing that he's not going anywhere until we're both ready, I snuggle back into him and allow myself to drift off to sleep.

My shift at Angel's today has been relatively dead. Most of the people who come in here during the day are on their lunch break so they can catch up on the sports and news that Angel always keeps running in here.

Melody, Mr. Stern's secretary, is here today. Thankfully she's not in my section. She's so nosey, and I don't need her knowing any more of my business than she already does.

As I'm cleaning a table, my attention is instantly jerked to one of the televisions at the mention of Ace's name.

A tall, blond news reporter pulls the microphone close to her lips and rattles off breaking news about the missing rock star. "Earlier this week an anonymous tip was e-mailed to Jane Ann Rogers's address, listed on the reward website, that Ace White is indeed alive and well. The e-mail also went on to say, and I quote, that Mr. White left over creative control differences with his band and has sought out legal counsel to advise him on the best way return to his career without facing lawsuits.

"Police are still unsure of the validity of this tip because the reward for information leading to Mr. White is now up to fifty thousand dollars. Law enforcement officials are busy sorting through over twenty-five hundred possible leads they've received since the reward value was increased. They are hoping to narrow down any legitimate leads that may come from them.

"That's all the information we have at this point. If investigators are able to narrow down who sent the tip from the IP address, they may have some helpful information on the case. If anything changes, I will be the first to report it. This is Linda Bronson for *Celebrity Pop Buzz Nightly's* daily update."

My jaw hangs open as I stare at the commercial on the screen.

Shit. Does that mean they are close to finding Ace? I need to tell him about this. He probably has no idea since we don't get cable or Internet in Willow Acres.

I dig my phone out of my back pocket but can't make myself dial the number. If I tell him this and they aren't anywhere close to finding him, I will have sent Ace running for no reason.

The only thing is, the e-mail was pretty spot-on, and very few people know that information. One of them is sitting in this bar at this very moment.

I turn my gaze on Melody, who instantly spots me marching in her direction and all the color drains out of her face.

"Did you have anything to do with this?" I glare at her, waiting for an answer.

She vigorously shakes her head, laying money down for her bill, trying to get out of here as quickly as possible.

When Melody stands up, I grab her wrist, forcing her to look me in the eye. "He trusted you. Is money really worth hurting someone who came to you for help? He just wants a normal life. Don't you understand that? He's trying to grieve and get his shit together and you just screwed him."

Melody's mouth drops open, but she doesn't say a word to defend her actions, which only infuriates me more. Anger pulses through my veins and I dig my fingers into her skin, causing her to grimace.

"Ouch, Iris. Let go. You're hurting me." There's a whimper in her voice, and it's wrong of me to put my hands on her like this, but

I can't help myself. She can't just screw with Ace's life like this and get away scot-free.

She's a coward—one that would do anything for money, apparently—and that pisses me off.

I squeeze harder. "Good. You're lucky I've got enough willpower to keep from punching you in the face."

"Let's be rational here," Melody pleads. "You hit me and I'll press charges."

"That might just be worth it," I growl.

"Will it be worth it to bring the cops around you and Ace? Think about it, Iris. You're a smart girl. Take your hands off me before you do something foolish."

Damn it. I hate that she's right. I glance around, and every eye in the bar watches us intently. I'll be damned if I'm the one who blows Ace's cover by being forced to explain what our little altercation is about.

I turn my gaze back to Melody. "If you mention one more thing about Ace, we will have a problem, and no threats of setting the police after me will stop me. Are we clear?"

She nods stiffly and then works herself free from my grip before she flees from the bar without saying another word to me.

Shit. What am I going to do?

I should turn Melody in and get her fired, but then that might make Mr. Stern call the police to question things, and I can't have any more attention brought down on us.

I take a deep breath as I fight the urge to rush out into the parking lot to take out my frustration on her for ruining my and Ace's plans, but before I can do that, Birdie's voice pulls me out of my thoughts.

"What was that all about?" she asks. "Things looked tense as hell over here."

I shake my head. I hate keeping secrets from my best friend, but this isn't my secret to tell. "Nothing. A misunderstanding. It was nothing."

Birdie nods slowly as she raises her eyebrows. "All right. Well, your order for table three is up."

"Thanks," I say as I fight the dread of knowing that soon my happy little world with Ace may come crumbling down.

ACE

Over the next month I quickly find myself in a comfortable routine with Iris. We spend every night wrapped in each other's arms, professing our deepest love to one another after intense bouts of lovemaking while making plans for our future together.

Most nights I read to her. She seems to really enjoy that, and it pleases me immensely just knowing we share a love of so many things.

In the evenings, we practice singing. Sometimes I join in and we do duets so she can get comfortable singing with a partner. It's in those moments that I have to combat jealous thoughts from running amok in my head. The idea of a man singing love songs to her drives me insane. Telling her I love her is my job, not some random dickwad's who gets on stage with her.

The daytime is the worst for me. Working out with basic push-ups and running can only last so long. I've fixed every broken window in the park, with the exception of that asshole Jeremy's place. That asshole loves to stare me down every chance he gets, so I'll be damned if I go out of my way to help him.

I've gotten so used to having Iris around that I find myself lonely when she goes to work most of the day. I like having her here with me, but I would never discourage her from going. I completely understand her need to prove her independence and take care of the trailer park that's been in her family for generations.

I've offered to help her, and I've made it clear many times that when the time comes, if she's short, I will give her the rest. I don't want to see her lose this place. It would break her heart, and I'm finding myself quickly becoming attached to the residents here myself, especially Adele. She's the one person around this park who I know will give it to me straight, and always threatens me with violence if I hurt Iris in any way, making me adore her even more for being so protective.

I adjust myself on the couch as I go back to working on the song that's been worming its way into my brain for most of the day. I stare at the words on the notebook paper and begin to sing them. "Love's like a tragedy. Look what it's done to you and me . . ."

Soon after I begin jotting more ideas down, the slam of a car door out front causes my heart to race. I shove myself off the couch and make my way outside to greet Iris just as I've been doing daily.

Her coat is pulled tightly around her as the January chill cuts through with a gust of wind. It's nearly five thirty and already it's dark. Thankfully the outdoor lights keep the lots lit up pretty well, but wintertime in Ohio is always the most depressing time of year.

Iris scowls at me as I stand on the front porch of my trailer as she approaches. "Where's your coat? It's freezing out here."

I laugh and continue to shiver in my short-sleeve shirt as she folds herself into my waiting arms. "I was anxious, and besides, I knew your love would warm me up."

She laughs and rolls her eyes. "You're crazy."

I open my mouth to answer when a shout from the trailer across the way catches my attention. "Hey, pretty boy! Don't think I've forgot about you."

I glance over to find Jeremy standing with a couple other guys around a trash barrel with a burning fire in it. A smug smile fills his face as he sets his eyes on me and takes a long pull from his beer.

I knew that asshole wouldn't let things go after I laid my hands on him the first time. He's the type of guy who looks for trouble and welcomes it. Honestly, I'm surprised it's taken this long for him to taunt me openly instead of just giving me dirty looks like he has been. Having guys with him who he thinks will have his back probably has a lot to do with it. I shake my head, unwilling to entertain him any further.

I throw my arm protectively around Iris's shoulders and turn to lead her inside. "Come on."

"That's it. Run inside like the little bitch you are." His taunts continue and the two men with him laugh. "Save some of that sweet pussy for me. I've been waiting for months now to tap that!"

I clench my fists and grit my teeth, and I can't stop myself from turning in Jeremy's direction. This fucker needs to be taught a lesson in manners. You don't speak to a woman like that. Ever.

I lunge forward but Iris shoves her hand into my chest, halting me. "Let it go. He's an asshole."

"I can't," I growl. "I can't just let him talk about you like that and get away with it."

"Yes, you can," she whispers harshly. "Forget him. We don't need to draw any attention to you right now."

My chest heaves as anger still pulses through me. I flick my gaze from Iris to Jeremy and to Iris's face and then shove my fingers into my hair and sigh. This is taking every inch of willpower I have to not hop off this porch and shove my fist in his smug face.

"Please," she says. "He's not worth it."

Her eyes plead with me to think about things rationally—to let it go. She's right. I don't need my plans to get fucked now that we've got our lives together mapped out. As soon as the taxes are taken care of in a few weeks, I'll head to California and she'll head for New York, getting shit done so we can be together permanently.

I nod, knowing she's right. I throw my arm back around her, leading her inside.

"See you later, Iris!" Jeremy shouts before all the men laugh together, causing me to clench my jaw as I slam the door shut.

I lean back against the door and shut my eyes, attempting to calm myself down to keep from rushing back out there and tearing Jeremy limb from limb.

Iris leans into me and then wraps her arms around my waist. "You did the right thing. Those guys are bad news."

"Fuck those guys. They don't scare me," I blurt out, not wanting Iris to think I'm weak. "I already beat Jeremy's ass once, and I'd do it again with ease."

"I don't doubt that you'd beat him in a fair fight, but three on one . . . they won't fight fair."

She's right, but the tension in the air is so thick that I can practically feel it on my skin. Jeremy's messing with me, and it's only a matter of time before this all comes to a head, because I won't let him do that again and get away with it. It's not in my nature to remain calm for long in situations like I was just in.

Iris leans back and grabs my hand, pulling me toward the couch. When I flop down on it, she crawls behind me and massages my shoulders. I close my eyes as her magical fingers dig into the tense muscles around my neck, trying to get me to relax.

I sigh. "Shouldn't I be the one massaging you? You're the one who worked all day."

She continues to work on me. "I think you need it more than I do right now. I'm hoping this will take your mind off the jerks across the street."

"You're right. The distraction is nice." I lean back into her. "Tell me something good about your day."

"Well . . ." she trails off. "I made nearly two hundred dollars in tips today."

"That's great news!" I tell her, excited. "How close are you now to reaching your goal of twenty thousand?"

"If everyone pays their rent on time next week, I'll have nearly twelve thousand dollars."

I turn around and kiss her lips. "I'm so proud of you. We'll figure out the rest when the time comes."

She shakes her head, causing her brown hair to fall over her shoulders into her face as she stares down at me. "I want to earn this on my own. I don't want to be your charity case."

I stare into her green eyes. "You know it wouldn't be like that. I would give you anything I have if you need it."

She runs her fingers across my jawline. "And I love you for that, but if I take money from you, it'll be a loan. I'll pay you back every dime."

"Iris—" I begin to argue but she cuts me off with a pointed look. "Fine. A loan it is, but there will be no interest and there are no time limits on paying it back."

Iris smiles and kisses my lips. "Now that I'll agree to."

We spend the rest of the night negotiating the terms of our looming arrangement and planning more of our future, and I do my best to pretend that I've forgotten Jeremy, even though what he said about Iris still causes my blood to boil every time I allow my mind to think about it.

IRIS

He has absolutely nothing in this kitchen to eat. If I didn't know better, I'd say the guy lived on leftover pizza and beer, because that's all I see in his entire place that's edible.

"Mornin'," Ace says as he comes from the back hallway, stretching and wearing nothing but a pair of black boxer-briefs.

I smile as I appreciate the view of his toned body and bite my lower lip. Everything about the guy is absolutely delicious—his hair, his breathtaking eyes, heart-stopping smile, and that sexy V that cuts in his hips just below his ripped abs. God absolutely smashed the mold when he made him.

"Hey. I hope you don't mind. I was looking for something to fix us for breakfast, but all you seem to have in here are old leftovers."

He shakes his head and a lock of his bronze hair falls into his eye.

I brush it away as he wraps his arms around me. "Your hair is getting longer. Do you think it's time to cut it again so you stay incognito?"

He sighs. "It does need a trim. Maybe I'll do that today while you're at work. Do you happen to have any scissors I can borrow?"

"Of course. Come on, get dressed. Let's go to my place so I can feed you, and I'll get you those scissors."

It takes forever for us to get dressed because we can't stop touching, kissing, and fondling each other, but I guess that's what two people in love do when they can't get enough of each other.

A weird calm fills the air as we finally make it outside—a feeling like everything is about to change.

The moment we round the corner, I spot the door of my trailer wide open. A chill runs down my spine. Without waiting for Ace, I break into full speed, running toward the doorway. I place my foot on the first step of my porch, and before I can climb up, Ace grabs the back of my coat, effectively yanking me back and not allowing me inside.

"I'll go first. Whoever did this could still be in there," Ace orders firmly and then steps between me and the door. "Stay put."

I open my mouth to protest, but the warning flashing in Ace's eyes tells me that this isn't up for negotiation. "Fine, but please hurry. I have to know what's missing."

After a quick peck on my forehead, Ace leaves me and then heads inside. "Jesus," he mutters as he steps inside.

"What? How bad is it?" I question while lingering outside the door as my heart leaps into my throat.

The sound of things toppling over pushes my patience to the brink and I can no longer contain myself from going inside to assess the damage.

I fly up the two wooden steps onto my tiny porch and then make my way inside. My heart drops to my feet as soon as my eyes roam over the scene before me, and I suck in a quick breath. It looks like a tornado went through the place. There's stuff everywhere. The couch has been flipped forward, resting on its front, along with Gran's favorite recliner, which has been pushed over and ripped down the back like someone took a knife and sliced through the fabric.

I shove my hands into my hair, pushing it off my forehead. I spin around, surveying the damage, and then turn to stone. "No. No. No."

"What?" Ace asks as he notices my stare fixed on the open freezer door in the kitchen. "Iris?"

I run over, stepping on the half-thawed food boxes that've been thrown down on the kitchen floor. The freezer is completely empty. My hands shake as I immediately drop to my knees, searching frantically for a sandwich baggie that was filled with all the money I had earned from tips since I started at Angel's a month ago.

This isn't happening to me!

Clear plastic pokes out from under one of the boxes, and I grab it and find myself staring at an empty bag. My heart immediately drops to my stomach, and tears burn before they begin falling down my cheeks. A scream tears from my throat. I push all of my anger into it, making it so loud that I'm sure the entire trailer park is wide-awake now.

"Iris?" Ace bends down next to me, concern filling his voice. "What is it?"

"It's gone," I'm barely able to whisper through my sobs. "All of it—the money I've been saving for the taxes. It's all gone."

Ace rubs his forehead and closes his eyes. "You kept it all here?"

I cry harder at my own stupidity, for trusting that the money would be safe here if I hid it. "I switched banks when I moved to New York, and the closest Wells Fargo bank is in Columbus, so I didn't make the drive to deposit it. My check from Angel's is direct deposit, so I never had to worry about that."

"Did you tell anyone that you had that money in there?" he asks.

I shake my head as I wipe my face with the back of my hand. "No. No one. I can't think of anyone—"

I cut myself off before I can finish that statement, because someone instantly pops into the forefront of my mind. The same guy who gave us problems last night and saw us go into Ace's trailer. Jeremy knew I wasn't here last night and used that knowledge to rob me blind.

Ace's nostrils flare and his jaw muscle flexes beneath his skin. "I'm going to kill that motherfucker."

He begins to stand, but I grab his wrist, keeping him kneeling on the floor next to me. "No. Ace. Don't risk it. It's not worth it."

Anger burns in Ace's eyes as he cradles my face in his hands and locks his gaze with mine. "No one is going to hurt you, Iris. No one. I'm getting your money back."

He crushes his lips to mine before standing so quick that I don't have a chance to grab him again to make him stay.

"Ace!" I yell as he whips out the door.

I scramble to my feet to chase after him, but he's already in a full sprint and nearly at Jeremy's door already. I call his name again, but he doesn't turn around. He's too pissed and is focused on righting the wrong that's been done to me.

A thunderous crack sounds across the graveled lot of the trailer park and I watch in complete horror as Ace kicks open Jeremy's door and rushes inside.

"What the fuck—" Jeremy shouts, but he doesn't get to finish his sentence before there's a booming crash inside.

My legs pump faster, burning with each step, as the need to stop Ace from doing something crazy overwhelms me.

I make it to the door of Jeremy's trailer in time to see Ace on top of Jeremy and landing a hard right to his face. I cringe as Jeremy's head snaps left.

"Where is it? Where's the money?" Ace screams in his face.

Ace yanks Jeremy up, expecting an answer, but a sharklike smile stained with blood fills Jeremy's face. "You'll never get it. That money's long gone."

Ace opens his mouth to say something else, but Jeremy spits and it lands under Ace's right eye, causing Ace to go into a frenzy. He lands blow after blow onto Jeremy's face as I stand there completely frozen with fear.

Jeremy's body goes limp under Ace, but he doesn't stop. No longer am I worried about the media finding him, but what will happen to him once the police get involved with this.

Blind rage overtakes Ace, and he doesn't show any signs of regaining control of himself without someone intervening. It's like he can't see that Jeremy's had enough, so I scream. "Ace! Stop! You'll kill him!"

I'm scared out of my mind because of the sheer intensity of the situation. I've never seen anyone lose it like that before, and it makes me think twice about taking off with Ace somewhere. This is the second time I've seen him go after Jeremy. It's clear that Ace isn't afraid to unleash his wrath on someone who angers him. This really drives it home that we haven't known each other that long. Love is blinding, so I've allowed myself to overlook that fact.

Suddenly, I find myself at a crossroad. The time has come to leave everything behind and run away with him, but I'm not sure I can do it like I promised. I wish I had more time to get to know him before I am forced into making a choice.

At the sound of my words, Ace stops his drawn-back fist from coming down yet again, his breathing erratic as he stares down at the unconscious man below him.

I rush to Ace's side and grab his arm, doing my best to hold him back. "He's not worth it."

Ace's viselike grip loosens and he allows Jeremy's limp body to fall to the dirty trailer floor. Ace turns to me with wide eyes and a panicked expression after he realizes the reality of what he's just done. He stares up at me. "What have I done?"

I'm not sure if he's looking for me to actually answer as he processes the situation for himself. Ace stands and stares up at the ceiling like he's trying to wrap his head around what's happened while he keeps repeating the word no over and over.

I reach down and press two fingers to Jeremy's throat. "He's still breathing, but he's in bad shape. He's going to need—"

Sirens scream in the far-off distance, causing the blood in my veins to run ice-cold. If Ace gets caught . . . I shake my head, not even wanting to think about it if that happens.

I stare up at Ace's conflicted face and press my lips to his. "Go."

His brow furrows as he stands over me. "Iris, I can't leave you."

"If you don't go now, things are going to get so much worse for you. You have to get out of here and let me handle this. You have to go before . . ." I find myself getting choked up as I implore the man I desperately love to leave me. "Just, please, Ace. Go."

"Iris . . . I won't—"

"Go!" I shout again.

He shakes his head. "No! Not without you."

"Get out of here!" I can see now that he's not going to listen to me, so I stand up and shove my hands into his chest as hard as I can. "Leave!"

He furrows his brow. "Why are you doing this? Don't push me away."

It's in that moment I do something I instantly wish I can take back. I lie. I lie to protect him in the only way I know that will convince him to leave me.

I close my eyes and take a deep breath to harden my face before redirecting my gaze on him. "I'm not going with you, Ace. I don't even really know you."

Hurt etches into his beautiful features, and it pains me to know that I'm causing him pain, but I know I need to do this for his own good.

"But you promised," he whispers.

"How can I ever trust that you won't lash out at me? You've obviously got issues. I can't give up my life for someone that I don't trust not to take their anger out on me someday." Tears run down my cheeks as I know the words I'm telling him are cutting like a knife, but it's the only way I know that will make him leave—that will ultimately keep him safe for now. I can't bear the thought of him being hauled out of here in handcuffs.

"Iris . . . this looks bad, I know, but I would never . . ." He swallows and closes his eyes like it hurts too much to even look at me. "I would never hurt you."

I take a deep breath, fighting back the urge to break down and say to hell with everything and run away with him anyway. I don't want to hurt him, but what choice do I have?

I square my shoulders and stare into his eyes. "I don't want to be with you."

He pauses for a beat and tears run down his face. "This changes things," he whispers. "If you don't want me, I'll go. I'll leave you like you're asking, but just remember, you did this. You tore us apart. I never wanted to be without you, and I would take my own life before I laid a finger on you. I don't know how you would believe I would do anything to you other than give you the world."

I choke back a sob and force a stern face, fearing if he doesn't go soon, I won't be able to pretend like this isn't absolutely gutting me. *"Go!"*

Ace doesn't immediately run off like I expect. Instead he leans in and kisses my forehead and murmurs, "I'll love you forever."

Then he turns his back to me and runs out the door, not giving me a chance to break down and beg him to stay.

The engine of his bike roars to life moments later, and I close my eyes, knowing that the man I love has just ridden out of my life as quickly as he came into it.

I collapse onto the floor, tears streaming freely as the realization hits me that I might not ever see Ace again after this. I don't want this to be the end of us. One day, I'll have to find him and explain—beg for his forgiveness for the hurtful lies I told him in order to keep him safe.

When the cops show up I'm curled into a ball, sobbing, next to a still-breathing but unconscious Jeremy. I didn't have the strength to move as my heart shattered into a million pieces.

"Miss? Miss, are you hurt?" I blink slowly a few times and then turn my gaze up at the young, dark-haired police officer leaning over me. "Can you tell me who did this to you?"

"Easy there," he says as I push myself up onto my elbow, and the officer places his hands on my shoulders, like I'm a broken flower.

"Tell me, miss, who did this, so we can go after them," he says again, but I shake my head, causing him to furrow his brow. "You don't know who did it?"

Jeremy's groan behind me pulls my attention to where the paramedics have somehow revived him and are busying themselves with checking him over.

"Where is that fucker?" Jeremy mumbles, and I cringe, knowing immediately that he obviously didn't get hit hard enough to forget that Ace was here.

The cop turns his attention away from me to Jeremy. "Who did this to you, sir?"

"That asshole, Ace. He lives in the trailer next to the office. He broke in here and attacked me."

The cop writes down some information on a notepad. "Do you know his last name?"

"Fuck no," Jeremy mutters as the medic helps him sit up before cleaning the lacerations above his eye.

I let out a breath slowly, relieved that at least he doesn't know Ace's last name, and just as I think we're in the clear of Ace getting out of this situation without being named, Jeremy's green eyes lock on mine and his face contorts in anger.

He points his long, slender finger in my direction. "Ask her his last name. She's fucking him."

I gasp just as every pair of eyes snaps onto me.

Oh. Shit.

The young cop who was once so concerned about me now stares at me through narrowed eyes. "Miss, I'm going to need you to come with me. I need to ask you a few questions."

I reluctantly nod and push myself to my feet and follow the cop out Jeremy's door. Suddenly it hits me that the best defense is a good offense. I need to try to make this police officer understand that Ace isn't the monster that Jeremy's bruised-up face makes him out to be.

Once we are by the car, the officer turns to me. "I'm Officer Rugger. Your name?"

"Iris Easton."

He writes that down. "Tell me what happened here *exactly.*"

I swallow hard. "It started a couple of months ago . . ."

I go into great detail about how Jeremy got rough with me a couple of months ago and Ace stepped in to defend me. The officer takes diligent notes of my account as I go on to tell him about Jeremy's taunting last night and how we discovered my place ransacked this morning.

Officer Rugger raises his eyebrows as he stares down at me. "I'll need to see your place and question Jeremy about his involvement in the burglary in question. It's imperative that I locate Ace. I'll need to confirm your story, and it's likely that Jeremy Winkler is going to press charges."

"I . . . um . . ." I hesitate, not wanting to give any information on Ace but knowing that it's not going to be possible if the cop keeps pressing me.

"His name, Ms. Easton." The irritated tone in the cop's voice doesn't go unnoticed by me.

I don't like being forced to reveal Ace's last name. Even though that's not public information, it's still not a good idea for me divulge anything that can be traced back to him, but since Johnson isn't what the public knows him as, it might not stir up any trouble.

I stare up at the young Officer Rugger and sigh. "It's Ace Johnson."

He stops writing. "He's not by chance the same Ace Johnson who's also known as Ace White, is he? The press wasn't privy to the star's real name, but it was told confidentially to the officers in Columbus and surrounding areas."

I raise my brow. I thought no one knew his name. Ace has no clue about this, I'm sure. He needs to know. As soon as all these people clear out, I'll call him and let him know, even though I'm sure I'm the last person he wants to talk to, considering what I just said to him.

I debate lying to the cop if it would give Ace more time to get away, but ultimately decide against it because I don't want to end up in jail for not complying with the law.

I nod and Officer Rugger's mouth drops open while his eyes grow wide and he reaches for the radio on his shoulder, clicking the button to call in to the police station. "Base, do you copy? This is

Rugger. I have a possible sighting of the missing person Ace Johnson, aka Ace White."

There's silence on the radio, and then the female dispatcher confirms the information that Officer Rugger just gave her.

The officer surveys the trailer park and then returns his gaze to me. "This is a pretty good place to hide out—no cable. No Internet. He couldn't have picked a place more back in time on modernization. No wonder he came here." He shakes his head before refocusing on me. "Ready to show me your place?"

I spend the next few hours going over again the story of how I met Ace and what occurred last night, leading to the fight today. Somehow the news of Ace being here leaks to the press and reporters swarm the trailer park almost immediately.

After the cops leave, the reporters stay put, surrounding my place and Ace's, yelling my name and asking questions every time I open the front door. I pace back and forth inside my trailer, scared out of my mind that I've just managed to make things much worse for Ace by verifying his last known residence. This is exactly what he was afraid would happen.

I stare out my kitchen window and laugh when I see one of the reporters knock on Adele's door only to get beaten when a broom-wielding Adele answers, shooing them off her property. She's obviously not talking.

Wish I could say the same about all the other neighbors.

Reporters line the gravel street that stretches down the middle of the trailer park, separating the trailers into two neat rows. All of the camera crews flood into the road, talking to any residents in the park willing to dish out a little dirt.

A persistent knock on my front door catches my attention, and I do my best to ignore it, but this person refuses to give up.

Angry with the way they keep trying to intrude into my personal life, I rush over to the door and yank it open. "What?"

"Jesus, Iris. Chill." Birdie holds her hands up.

I reach out, grab her jacket, and yank her inside. "Get in here."

I slam the door behind her and then lean against it, closing my eyes, wishing this nightmare was over and life would return to the way it was a couple of weeks ago. Before all this madness came down on us—back when Ace was blissfully hiding from the rest of the world here with me.

It hits me then that this is the madness that Ace was trying so hard to protect me from. He knew this was going to be bad. He knew it would be just like this.

"What the hell happened here?" Birdie asks, glancing around my trashed trailer. "Were you robbed?"

I nod. "Ace thinks Jeremy did it."

Birdie raises her hand to her face. "Oh. My. God. Did Ace kill Jeremy? Is that why all the reporters are here?"

I roll my eyes. "No, but he did beat him up pretty good. They hauled Jeremy off in an ambulance, but he seemed fine, if you ask me. He went out of his place cussing up a storm, yelling to anyone who would listen that he was going to sue Ace's ass."

She furrows her brow. "That's it? Why all the reporters then for a fight?"

I sigh. "I might as well tell you now. The secret's out."

"What secret?" She tilts her head, making her blond hair fall to one side.

"Ace . . . he's . . . well . . . you know that missing rock star the world seems to be searching for?"

"Yeah . . . Iris, I'm confused."

"Ace is the missing rock star," I blurt out.

Her dark brown eyes widen. "Wait a minute. You're telling me that Ace is Ace White of Wicked White?" I nod and Birdie squeals. "Are you sure? How long have you known?"

"Whoa." I laugh. "Slow down."

"I can't help it," she retorts excitedly. "It's not every day that your best friend dates a rock star who's been in hiding from the entire world in her trailer. I mean, it sucks that all the reporters are here, but it's an amazing situation."

So we sit down at my kitchen table and I tell her . . . *everything*. It feels good to finally be able to tell someone just how much I love Ace and what he means to me. I would like to believe that this will be just a small road bump for us, but honestly, after how I just treated him, I wouldn't be surprised if Ace hates me.

I know lying about not trusting him enough to leave with him had hurt him, but I did it to save him from this chaos, since he wasn't ready to be found yet.

"That day at Angel's—with Melody—she's the anonymous tipster, isn't she?" Birdie asks.

I nod. "Yeah. I'm almost positive it was her."

"Do you think she did it because she wanted the reward money?"

"What reason would she have other than that?" I ask. "She really didn't stand to gain anything else."

"That's fucked up," she says, and then she pauses for a beat. "Besides all that . . . how was the sex with Ace?" A fierce blush floods my cheeks, causing her to giggle. "That good, huh?"

I nod. "It was . . . gah! Amazing. I mean, he's so romantic, and he actually loves to quote Shakespeare."

My mind drifts off to what the good times with Ace were like. A weight settles over my heart and presses down at the thought that I may never have those with him again.

Birdie rests her chin in her hand as she stares at me with a huge grin on her face. "He actually *quotes* Shakespeare?" I blush and nod. "Wow. He's like the perfect man for you, Iris. He's all artsy and deep and shit. Kind of makes me feel bad for believing he was some outlaw serial killer." She sighs and there's an odd flicker of sadness in her eyes. "What are you two going to do now?"

I lean back in my chair. "I hurt him bad, Birdie. He's not going to forgive me easily. And to make matters worse, I have no clue where he is or how to even start looking for him. I don't know if I'm ever going to get the chance to apologize."

Birdie stretches her arm across the table and takes my hand. "When things cool down, he'll come back for you. He'll come to his senses eventually and realize that you said what you did to save him."

I give her hand a squeeze. "I hope so."

Chapter 23

CELEBRITY POP BUZZ NIGHTLY

A panoramic view of Willow Acres Mobile Home Community shows all the dilapidated trailers set in two neat rows with a gravel road separating them before the camera focuses on its star reporter. Her blond hair shifts in the slight breeze as she smiles and gazes directly into the lens.

"Good evening, America. This is Linda Bronson coming to you live from the sleepy little town of Sarahsville, Ohio, where this small community has just been rocked with the revelation that they've had a celebrity hiding out among them for months. That's right, we've confirmed that Ace Johnson, also known as Ace White, has been living in this run-down trailer for the past three months, mixing among the locals and even working as a handyman. It's unknown why Ace picked this location, but one thing is clear, he did not want to be found.

"The police tracked Ace to this trailer park after a nine-one-one call came into the local authorities here reporting a disturbance at the residence across the street, owned by one Jeremy Winkler. There appears to have been an altercation between Mr. Winkler and Ace White, who fled the scene before the police arrived. Allegedly, Mr. White has been involved in a romantic affair with the owner of this mobile home community, Iris Easton"—the screen flips to video of Iris walking to her trailer, attempting to block her face from the camera, and repeating *no comment*—"but so far Ms. Easton has refused to issue an official statement about her relationship with Ace White.

"Wicked White's tour manager, Jane Ann Rogers, did tell us that she's ecstatic that there has been an update in Mr. White's disappearance and wants to implore Ace to reach out to her, allowing her to help him with whatever struggle he's going through.

"As always, when we discover any additional information, we will bring it to you live. For *Celebrity Pop Buzz Nightly*, I'm Linda Bronson."

24

ACE

Staring at the four walls of my hotel room is beginning to drive me mad. I can't turn on the television without seeing my face plastered all over the news. I knew once they got wind of where I'd been hiding and who I was with, it would turn into a circus. Jane Ann is probably reveling in all the press my situation is creating for the band. She likes anything that makes money.

Iris's face has also been plastered everywhere, and I feel guilty about that. I didn't want her relationship with me to cause problems for her career, and I'm afraid there's no going back now. It seems that she's quickly becoming a household name, seeing as she's the last known link to me.

God. I fucking miss her like crazy.

I can't believe she would even entertain the idea that I could *ever* hurt her. I love her. I would rather rip my own soul out and hand it over to Satan himself before I caused her one ounce of pain. I've thought about going back so many times to make her understand that, but I know that I can't just waltz back into her trailer and force her to be with me.

The truth is, Iris's words really hit home. I do have a temper problem. It's something that's plagued me my entire life. When it comes to protecting someone I care about, I lose all rationality, and that sometimes makes me look like an unstable individual. I'm getting better controlling myself, but I'm still a work in progress, so I understand why she's scared of. She has every right to feel that way after the way I ripped into Jeremy and the guy that pawed her at the bar—the one she had no clue about, thank God. That wouldn't have helped my case any.

Iris has called my cell a few times, but I can't bring myself to talk to her. I can't bear the thought of hearing her apologize for rejecting me and then maintain her stand of not wanting me. It would crush me even more, and I may not be able to recover from knowing for a fact that I'll never have another shot with her.

She said it point-blank that she doesn't trust me. That's pretty hard to misinterpret. Her words about not wanting me anymore fucking stung and sent me into a dark depression.

I've spent the last three weeks in this hotel debating what my next move should be, because honestly, I just haven't had the will or drive to go on. My story is the hot topic of conversation. Everyone seems to be looking for me now that it's been confirmed that I'm alive and well, just hiding. Hell, it makes me paranoid to leave this room for very long for fear of being discovered, but it's obvious that I can't run forever. Sooner or later I'm going to have to deal with things.

There're so many damn things I need to face that I don't even know where to start.

The police are still looking to question me about the fight I had with Jeremy, so there's that whole mess, which I'm sure will result in me going to court. Jane Ann has been all over television and social media pleading with the public to give her information and claim the fifty-thousand-dollar reward if she finds me. Some people would sell their own mother for that much dough, which is why I need to be more careful than ever. I don't know why I ever thought running away from everything would make things easier. I know I'm a highly intelligent man, but taking off wasn't very smart on my part. It's only made shit ten times harder.

I wish Iris was here. I wish I could hold her. I wish things could go back to how they were a few weeks ago, when we were still together, still anonymous.

I lie back against my pillow and turn on the news channel, hoping to catch a glimpse of her face, and I'm shocked when I see her sitting across from Linda Bronson, that same reporter who has been stalking me since Mom died. The woman makes her living digging into the lives of celebrities that the public is dying to know about.

I didn't realize at the time what a media frenzy walking away from everything would create, but I felt like I didn't have any other options at the time. Mom was dying, and I was going to get to her, and no one was going to stop me.

I sit up on the edge of the bed and stare at Iris's beautiful face. Her dark hair is pinned up, so I have a clear view of her mesmerizing green eyes. It's plain to see the pain in her eyes. It may not be clear to the general public, but I can tell she's hurting. It makes me want to believe that she didn't mean what she said about not wanting me anymore—that she still wants me—needs me, and that she's not afraid of me.

"Iris, thank you so much for agreeing to finally sit down and talk to me," Linda says with a sly smile on her face.

I don't trust that woman one fucking bit. I think she'd sell her soul if it meant getting the best story.

Iris doesn't say anything, just simply pulls her lips into a tight line and smiles politely.

"You've avoided telling your side of the story since the news broke about you and Ace White over three weeks ago, so why end your silence now?"

Iris slowly licks her lips and sits a little straighter in her chair. "I haven't had any contact with Ace since the day he left. Besides the fact that I'm missing him like crazy, I need to see him to apologize—to tell him I didn't mean some of the hurtful things I said."

My heart does a double thump against my ribs and I swallow hard. She misses me? Wants to apologize? Does this mean she still wants me?

"What did you say?" Linda probes, wanting more specifics about our fight.

Iris doesn't speak, just simply shakes her head. "That's not information that I'm willing to share."

Linda leans in, like she's really wanting to pick at poor Iris's brain. "Do you think he'll come back if he sees this, Iris?"

Iris shrugs. "I don't know, but I'm leaving Willow Acres soon. The state is going to seize my home due to unpaid taxes, so I'm going back to New York and, well . . . I guess I just wanted him to know, and this was the only way I knew that I might have a chance to reach him since he isn't returning any of my phone calls."

Linda's face morphs into a dreamy smile as the camera pans back to her. "It sounds like the two of you had quite the love affair. Tell me, Iris, do you love him?"

"Yes," she whispers, and warmth spreads through my chest as I find myself leaning toward the television. "I love him very much. I just want him to know that."

"I love you too, Iris," I say, even though I know she can't hear me, but wishing that she could.

"Let's hope Ace sees this and makes contact with you. We're all still worried about him," Linda tells Iris and then looks into the camera and signs off with her typical catch phrase.

As soon as the channel flips to a commercial, the same thought runs through my mind over and over—getting back to Iris.

I've been absolutely miserable without her, but she hurt me bad. On one hand I want to prove to her that she'll always be safe with me, but on the other I hate the fact that she's able to believe that I'm some kind of monster after how much I've opened up to her. The woman knows everything about me.

The more I replay the things Iris just said on TV, the more I find myself getting angry. If she loves me so much and misses me, why did she push me away? It's like she's the one making decisions about our relationship. She gets to determine when I need to be pushed away and hurt, and then it's also up to her when she gets to plead for me to come back by pronouncing publicly how much she loves me and that she's sorry. I don't like being someone's puppet. I don't like my feelings fucked with any old time someone feels like it.

She broke her promise to me about sticking by my side. Why isn't it up to me to decide if I can still love her? She shouldn't go on television and make me seem like an uncaring asshole who just ran off.

Besides, I don't know if I can I ever trust her again after all this. How will I know she means what she promises after that?

Does she mean what she just said in the interview about being sorry and missing me and loving me, or is she somehow using me for publicity after I tried so hard to protect her from that very thing?

So many fucking questions rattle through my brain.

It would be so easy to pick up the phone and call her—to hear the words straight from her mouth that she wants me back and have her explain why she pushed me away like she did, but I can't bring myself to do it. When I have any communication with her about what's going on between us, it needs to be face-to-face. I need to see her expression when I ask her if she still loves me. I need to see for myself that she means it and isn't bullshitting me for some fucking camera.

I flop back against the pillow and sigh heavily.

I shouldn't have gotten involved with her. It's complicated the hell out of everything.

It's hard knowing that the media are tormenting her with questions about my whereabouts, because I don't know if she's enjoying the attention or if it's beating her down the same way it does me. If it's interfering with her life, it makes me feel even worse for being a selfish bastard and taking her. I knew that this scenario was probable the moment she agreed to be with me. I pray the havoc I've released into her life doesn't affect her when she goes back to New York. The last thing I ever wanted was for her career to become overshadowed by the fact that she's been with me. Hell, it's already made national news, and the longer I keep holding out on facing my life, making everyone wonder where in the hell I am, the longer the press will continue to hound her.

Iris is so insanely talented and deserves every opportunity to achieve her dream without the likes of me tainting her chances.

But maybe if I fix things—clear the air with Mopar Records and Jane Ann—Iris might have a shot of getting out from under the press's microscope and not have Broadway completely ruined for her.

My eyes snap to the prepaid cell phone that I bought when I first started my undercover adventure. I could take all this pressure off Iris with one phone call, exposing myself to the world.

My palms sweat as I pick up the phone. This is the right thing to do. Everything has gotten out of hand, and it's time for me to fix it.

The moment I enter the numbers in and hit send, I close my eyes, waiting for the voice I've been dreading for the last four months to answer.

"Who is this?" Jane Ann's shrill voice snaps onto the line.

"It's me. It's Ace," I say. "I'm ready to talk now."

The moment I get past the security checkpoint exit at LAX I'm nearly blinded from all the camera flashes. In the middle of all the madness stands Jane Ann, wearing a smug smile that matches the flashy sequined black dress that's sure to attract attention from every angle. One of the security guys who usually accompanies Wicked White to events stands beside her, doing his best to keep the paparazzi away.

She holds her arms open wide to me and more flashes go off, all of the photographers hoping to catch our reunion on film. "Welcome home, Ace."

She's fucking unbelievable.

I shake my head and push past her, not willing to put on the show she wants for the cameras. I'm not here to answer questions or to gain the public's sympathy. I'm here to get my shit squared away.

Jane Ann follows close behind me, leading the trail of paparazzi our way. "Ace, at least give the camera a sympathetic smile."

"Screw that. You know I'm only back to get this all squashed. I could care less about how this will affect my career. I told you over the phone that I'm done being your puppet," I fire back.

The hulking security guard ushers us through the automatic doors leading outside and then into an awaiting black limo.

I slide inside and Jane Ann immediately follows, and we're shut in. The reporters shove their cameras up to the windows, attempting to get a shot of us inside the dark-tinted glass, but I refuse to give them much to report. I keep my head down with my sunglasses on, doing my best to hide my face.

As soon as the car pulls away from the curb, the weight of Jane Ann's heated stare hits me full force.

"What?" I ask in a harsh tone as I turn to face her, readying myself for her to start bitching at any moment.

Her blue eyes narrow at me. "Do you have any idea the hell you put us all through? I've had to work my ass off in order to convince Mopar that you've had some sort of mental break after it came out that you were alive and well."

"I don't give a shit about what you've been through. If you haven't noticed, I just buried the woman I consider to be my mother and I've been yanked away from the girl I love, so excuse me for not really giving a shit about what you've been through."

Jane Ann sighs. "Look, Ace. I'm sorry about that. I should've handled things a little differently, but you should've too. We both were wrong, and now we have to fix what we've screwed up. We have to make the label happy. The label is ready to sue, Ace. They lost a lot of money after nearly four months of canceled shows. The best thing you can do now is beg for the mercy of the public, claiming to have had a mental break over the death of—"

"No!" I assert with authority. "I will not use my mother as an excuse for walking away from everything. I left because I'm tired of being your fucking puppet. I'm sick of being something that I'm not."

Jane Ann scrubs her forehead with her hand, clearly flustered.

"What is it that you want, exactly? I mean, what was so bad that you felt like you had to walk away from everything in order to make your point? You're the star of the band. What more could you want?"

I laugh harshly. "Where do I even start? I hate everything Wicked White. I hate the kind of music I'm forced to sing. I hate the clothes I'm forced to wear. The way I'm paraded around and not allowed to refuse things that I'm not comfortable with. All so you can make a buck off me. You won't even give my ideas a chance."

"I'm doing what's best for you." Her face twists in anger. "If it weren't for me—"

"I'd still be in Ohio and happy," I quickly cut her off.

"No," she counters. "That's not true. You were hungry for a music career and you wouldn't have been happy until you got one. So, Ace, honey, you would've been in Ohio, still plugging away on that frivolous philosophy degree, dreaming about having a career like the very one you're on the verge of losing."

I lick my suddenly dry lips as the words from her mouth hit me as a possible truth. She's right. Dreaming about making it in the music industry was something I always did, and in truth, that's mostly why I agreed to signing a deal where everything was dictated to me. I knew going in that I would have absolutely no creative control, but I was hoping that would change over time—that Mopar would trust in my talent enough to give me a shot at writing and performing the kind of music I love.

In reality I'm what the industry refers to as an indie rock artist. I want to march to the beat of the soulful drum that moves me and not play this lame pop shit that I've been forced into.

"You're right," I whisper. "I hate admitting that, but you are."

Her eyes soften. "Ace, I know you want to write and perform your own music. I promise, if you stick with me and work through this little hiccup in the road, that I will make sure that you get to do more of that."

"You will?" I ask, surprised.

"Yes." She nods. "I'll do everything I can, since you're obviously so unhappy with the way things are going. I'm sorry about how I treated you before, and I'm asking you to trust me to guide you in the right direction, just like I have been over the past couple of years when I took your career to this level."

I bite the corner of my thumbnail as I think about what she said. Mr. Stern confirmed that my contract states that I'm still obligated to fulfill concert dates and record two more records, but he also said there was a clause in there allowing me to have creative control of my brand. I don't mind being on the road. Of course I'll miss Iris, but I know that the sooner I get my shit back in order, the sooner I can track her down and salvage what's left of our relationship.

"What do I have to do in order to save myself the headache of having to fight Mopar Records on a lawsuit for breach of contract?"

Jane Ann's mouth pulls up in a halfhearted smile. "We need to get your side of the story out there. I need you to be honest with the world—tell them you were upset over your foster mother and apologize—to *everyone*. I'll arrange a sit-down interview with Linda Bronson from *Celebrity Pop Buzz Nightly* since she's been following your story so close. If we get you seen, things will get back on the right track."

Two days later, after consulting with an attorney on what I should and shouldn't say, I sit down in an oversize white chair facing the reporter who gets under my skin like no other.

I unbutton my gray jacket and try to relax in the seat and pretend that the hot lights shining down on me like the blistering sun aren't causing me to sweat.

"Just try and be natural. Viewers tend to believe you more if you seem comfortable with what you're saying," Linda Bronson says as she double-checks her bright red lipstick, which stands out against her platinum-blond hair and black dress suit. "You'll want the viewers on your side if you're hoping to win back your fans' trust and get your career restarted."

I nod stiffly and roll my shoulders, attempting to force the tension out, because I do owe the fans an apology for standing them up. It was wrong of me to do that. I know I let a lot of them down.

"Linda, we're on in five," a woman standing just left of the camera tells her and then takes a step back, counting down from five.

Linda tosses her hair, plasters the biggest grin on her face, and sets her eyes directly on the camera lens focused on her. "Good evening, America. I'm Linda Bronson with *Celebrity Pop Buzz Nightly*, coming to you live from the California home of Ace White. You might remember Ace as being the front man of the famous band Wicked White, but what he's gained worldwide notoriety from is his recent disappearance. Many thought he had met with an untimely demise, while others like his tour manager, Jane Ann Rogers, held out hope that he was alive.

"I, myself, have been covering the story of Ace White's disappearance from the very beginning, following up on every lead, and I was getting nowhere. It wasn't until a domestic disturbance in an Ohio mobile home community was reported to authorities that Ace's whereabouts were discovered. He had been hiding out, living under his true name of Ace Johnson, working as a handyman. Today Ace White sits down to tell us his side of the story and just why he walked away from a successful career."

Linda turns to me with an over-the-top expression of pity in her eyes. "Thank you so much for being here with me, Ace."

I rub my sweating palms on my thighs and immediately see Jane Ann shaking her head. I freeze instantly and then simply rest my hands against my legs. "Thank you for having me, Linda."

"So, Ace, I'm going to get right down to it. Can you please tell us what happened on the day you walked out on a sold-out crowd?"

I lick my lips, not wanting to reveal the problems of my life to the world, but I know at this point I have no choice. "I received a phone call from a police officer in Columbus, where the woman who raised me lived. Sarah Johnson was my foster mother, and I loved her like she was my real mother; the state even allowed me to take on her last name as my own when I was sixteen. She wanted to adopt me, but we found out that if she did that, I would lose a lot of the state funding for my impending college education, so the state agreed to grant me the name change. In my eyes, that was just the same as her adopting me. It signified that we were really a family and that she thought of me as her son.

"Anyway, the officer told me that they had found Sarah unresponsive and had transported her to the Grant Medical Center in critical condition."

Linda clutches at her chest. "You poor dear! What happened after you got that call?"

"Naturally, I wanted to hop in my car and speed off to be with her. She was my only family, and I wanted to be there for her like she was for me while I was growing up. It was important to me to be there, so against the wishes of my bandmates, tour manager, and label, I took off."

"That's completely understandable. I think a lot of people would do the same thing if they were in your position." She tilts her head. "What was with the dramatics—flipping the band the middle finger before going on this hiatus? What caused that?"

I sigh, remembering what the lawyer told me to say—be truthful, but be sure to paint myself, the band, and the label in a positive light. "The band dynamics have been rocky for the past year. We've had some trouble coming together as a cohesive unit, and so when they immediately went off the deep end because shows needed to be canceled so I could be with my mom, something in me snapped." My attention jerks to Jane Ann, who nods and twirls her finger, indicating for me to continue discussing my "self-destruction."

"When you say you snapped . . . what happened?"

I clear my throat and continue. "I lost all focus, I guess. Everything around me seemed to be falling apart, and I felt like I was losing my identity with Wicked White, and the sudden news of my mother being gravely ill and then passing . . . it's like it all culminated at one time and I just sort of lost my head. Suddenly I just wanted away from everything. I wanted to be somewhere without all the pressures that come with being a rock star."

Linda crosses her legs. "So that's when you decided to cut your hair and shave your beard in order to go into hiding?"

I nod. "Yes. I wanted to be different so I couldn't be found. I started with a pair of scissors and created a new look that would be harder to recognize. I knew that Jane Ann and the media would continue to follow me after I flipped off the band and walked off stage, so I needed to throw them off my scent so I would have a chance of normalcy."

"Well, you look fantastic. The new look is amazing. Do you feel like a changed man now?"

"Most definitely."

"It's my understanding that you were involved with a certain young woman during your three-month period away from stardom. Can you tell us a little about Iris Easton?"

My heart squeezes at the mention of her name. Even though I'm still angry and hurt by the way she ended things between us, I refuse to drag her any further into the madness that is my life right now. I won't hurt her chances of landing a Broadway role on her own merits by publicizing our relationship any more than it's already been. I know how important it is to her to get a role. I don't want it to be another source of heartbreak for her if she gains a role, only to learn later on that she got it because of me and not because of her remarkable talent.

I shake my head. "I won't answer any questions pertaining to Ms. Easton."

Linda Bronson raises her eyebrows, like this surprises her, but she doesn't press me any more about Iris. "Okay, well, let's move on to the record label. Have you gotten a chance to speak with Mopar Records since your return a few days ago?"

"My tour manager, Jane Ann, has, yes."

"And what are they saying?" Linda probes.

I scratch the corner of my mouth, trying to ignore the dry-mouth feeling that's come over me since this interview started. "My contract still stands. The Wicked White shows that were canceled because of my absence will be rescheduled."

"Really? Just like that and you're back in the label's good graces? They aren't going to sue you?"

I shake my head. "I'm going to have to work really, really hard to prove to the label that mentally I'm back on track and that they can trust me. If I fulfill my contract, then there's no reason for them to seek legal action against me. I will, however, be exerting more creative control in the songs Wicked White produces, along with what songs we perform. I'll be leading the band in a new creative direction."

"Will you be sticking to the same type of songs that you've been producing?"

"No. We will be changing up the sound of Wicked White."

Linda leans over and lays her hand on my forearm. "I can't wait to see the direction you go in. Good luck, and I personally wish you the best in your future endeavors." She turns away from me and faces the camera again. "For *Celebrity Pop Buzz Nightly*, I'm Linda Bronson."

The camerawoman cuts the filming, and Linda's body visibly relaxes as she turns to me. "That was great. I wish you would've talked a little about Iris, but it was still good."

I shake my head as the sound woman reaches in my shirt and unhooks my microphone. "I don't want to drag her in this any more than I already have."

She nods. "Iris is such a sweet girl. That girl really loved you."

I don't miss the past-tense wording in that sentence. "You don't think she loves me anymore?"

Linda glances up at me as she leans forward so the sound technician can remove her mic pack from the waistband of her skirt. "Ace, honey, how much longer do you think she's going to wait around for you? The girl was desperate enough to find you that she allowed me to interview her, even though it was clear that she was uncomfortable. She truly didn't believe that she had any other way of reaching you, other than through begging for you to contact her on national television. She really put herself out there, and I'm going to bet that you still haven't called her."

I frown and my eyes dart down to the ground.

Linda sighs. "That's what I thought. Don't worry, though. She's a smart girl, and she'll realize that you were with her out of convenience and nothing more. I mean, my God, look at you. You're insanely attractive, and this new broken bad-boy image will drive the female fans wild. If I didn't know any better, I would say this was just a brilliant publicity stunt."

"It's not like that at all. I'm not . . . I didn't . . ." I shove my hand through my hair, frustrated that I can't even seem to communicate how I feel about Iris. I take a deep breath and let it out slowly between pursed lips. "I honestly doubt she wants me around, and if she does, I'm not sure I can take her back after what she said to me."

"Trust me. She wants you." Linda stands. "And if I were you, I wouldn't take too much time figuring that out. I imagine a girl like her won't stay single long. Some guy will snap her up in a heartbeat if she allows herself to get over you."

"Linda, we need to move on to the next location," the camerawoman calls, hurrying her star reporter along.

Linda nods and then gives me a sad smile. "Good luck, Ace. I hope you find whatever it is that you're looking for and that I don't have to go on any more wild chases across the country searching for you."

I swallow down the lump that's building in my throat as I think about how Linda might just have a point. Iris is a beautiful, intelligent woman who has the voice of an angel. Any man would be a fool if he didn't instantly fall for her like I did.

As bad as I want to rush back into her life, I know it's not fair if I can't give her a realistic timeline when all this label drama will be over. A few more days sorting things out and I'll go find her. I'll prove to her that I'm a good man—the kind who will cherish her forever. I'll show her that I can rein in my emotions and that I can keep myself in check.

Jane Ann steps up next to me with a huge smile. "That was perfect. You had the right emotion and gave just enough details without giving away too much. Gah! Linda Bronson was correct, this will be huge publicity for you."

"Jane Ann—"

She holds her hands up. "I know, I know. You don't care about that, but Ace, let's be realistic. Fans are going to eat up the whole tortured artist thing, and they'll be on pins and needles waiting to see what you're going to do next."

We walk out onto my back patio. February in California is nothing like Ohio. It's still warm enough to sit outside and enjoy the weather. The place is just as I left it a few months ago—perfectly landscaped, with tall shrubs providing all the privacy anyone could ever dream of. That's one plus about living in a gated community: it really cuts down on the random break-ins when you're not home.

"I want to get to work on the new songs right away. We need to call the band together so we can go over what our new sound will be."

"I still don't think changing the direction—"

I hold my hand up. "If I am going to stay in Wicked White, these are my terms, and if you want to stay on board and make money off of me like you're used to, then you'll stop fighting me on this."

"Okay, but the other guys might not like it," she says. "They signed up to play pop music that has mass appeal. They won't like doing a one-eighty with the sound and becoming a completely different-sounding band for fear they'll lose the fans that they've already amassed."

I shrug. "Then let them quit. They all hate me anyhow, so it might be nice to get some new blood in the band."

She opens her mouth like she's going to protest but then quickly closes it and nods. "Maybe you're right on that point. JJ can be a real prick at times. I hate having to deal with him myself. The other two will fall in line I think, once you assert more authority as the leader of the band."

"That's going to happen, or I'll find a new drummer and bassist, only this time I get a say if we replace them."

"Okay, any other demands?" she asks.

"Only one: I want to pay Willow Acres's taxes off for Iris. She's going to lose it soon if they aren't paid, and I want to do that for her. There are some amazing people who live there, and I don't want to see them lose their homes."

She tilts her head. "That brings up another subject: Jeremy Winkler. He's pressed assault charges, and that's something we're going to have to deal with."

I pinch the bridge of my nose. That douche bag is really a fucking thorn in my side. "We'll deal with it."

"I could offer to pay him off in order to get—"

"No. I refuse to give that asshole any money. If he sues me and wins—"

"Then that could be a lot more money in the long run. Let me have our attorneys settle with him out of court. It'll be a lot less messy and we'll have the matter over with a lot sooner." When I hesitate, Jane Ann adds, "Be smart about this, Ace. I know you want this all behind you, and paying him off is the best way to do that. Once we get through this, you can refocus on your career—your music—and figure out where your relationship stands with Iris Easton. Aren't those the most important things right now?"

"Yes," I answer immediately. "Iris and my music are the only things that matter to me."

"Then let me help you by doing this. I'll get the taxes paid off to help Iris, and then I'll figure out how much it'll take to get rid of Jeremy. It's the best way. Trust me."

I turn to her and take in Jane Ann's heart-shaped face, hoping that she really does have my best interests at heart as I agree to what she's saying. "Okay. If you and the attorneys think that's best, then okay. I need time to refocus on my music and find my soul again. It's going to take me some time to come up with new material for the next record. Will you call the band and set up a time we can all meet? I want to rip off that Band-Aid and get pissing them off over with."

"Yes. I'll make that happen right away." Jane Ann nods, pulling out her phone. "Let me know if you need anything else. I need you focused. Those new songs won't write themselves."

A calm comes over me, and for once I finally feel like I'm taking control of my career and my voice is being heard.

IRIS

The bustling sound of New York City out the window of my shoe-box apartment is a far cry from the quiet surroundings of my childhood home. It was hard leaving Willow Acres, but knowing that Adele and Birdie are running things in my absence helps me rest easier at night. Birdie has decided to hold off on moving here with me for now because she loves her night shift job at Angel's, and she knows I'm depending on her to help Adele with the trailer park. I trust both of them implicitly. They're my family—blood or not—and they're all I've got.

When I went to Tanner's office three days before my scheduled flight back to the city to tell him that I wouldn't be able to come up with the money for the taxes, I was shocked to find they had already been paid. I didn't figure Ace would still do that for me, considering I hadn't heard from him for at least three weeks at that point.

I went on national television, practically begging him to come back, or at the very least call me, but I never heard a peep from him. I find myself not only hurt by the fact that he didn't even make an attempt to contact me, but pissed. It makes me wonder if the romantic nice guy who made me lots of poetic promises was full of nothing but shit. I think after pouring my heart out in front of millions of people, I at least deserve a phone call, even if it is just to tell me things are over and to move on with my life.

So, needless to say, I was surprised that he'd followed through with helping me out by paying the taxes.

I've been working my ass off ever since then to save the money to pay him back. I have around two thousand dollars saved, and I will pay him back every penny . . . once I figure out how to get in contact with him, that is.

It's been a little over five weeks since I last saw Ace in person. Sure, I've seen him from time to time like the rest of America on the covers of tabloid magazines and on television when Linda Bronson updates her viewers on Ace's comeback. He never mentions me willingly. If my name is ever brought up in an interview, he refuses to comment, so I figure he's still hurt that I wouldn't leave with him.

"Are you nearly ready?" Darcy, my roommate, asks.

"Yes," I tell her as I finish the last coat of my mascara. "Let's go."

Darcy pulls her dark, curly hair into a ponytail, showing off her slender neck and perfectly round face, before grabbing her purse.

I follow her out the door and wait on her to lock up before we head to the elevator.

I met Darcy nearly a year ago when I first moved into the city. She and I worked together at Flows and immediately hit it off. Like me, Darcy moved here to make it in theater, but her dream is to be a prima ballerina. When I decided it was time to come back to New

York, she was the first person I called, and I have been crashing on her couch for the last two weeks.

I was ecstatic to get my old waitressing job back here at Flows. That place was like a second home to me, so I am grateful for the familiarity. Everything fell back into place just as it was a few months ago, and it's like I never left.

I pick at my nails, noticing I desperately need a manicure, but am determined to save every penny until Ace gets his money back.

"How'd your audition go yesterday?" I ask Darcy as we walk down the busy street on the way to work.

She shrugs. "They didn't seem superenthused by me, so I doubt I'll get a callback."

I nudge her shoulder with mine. "Don't be such a negative ninny. I'm sure you did fantastic."

"This is a tough, tough city to catch a break in. It's hard to always keep positive." She turns toward me. "Speaking of positive, are you ready for tomorrow?"

"As ready as I'll ever be. I'm ready to get back in the audition saddle. I think I've picked up a few new tricks over the last few months that will really help."

Darcy smiles at me knowingly. "Are we talking about the tips that a certain beautiful rock star gave you about connecting to the crowd?"

I blush and tuck a stray lock of hair from my ponytail behind my ear. "Yeah. He really helped me open up."

She laughs. "I bet he did."

I laugh too, but deep down, the overwhelming sadness that exists in my heart curls its way up into my chest. It hurts that I haven't heard from him. After everything we went through—the things we said and the promises we made to each other—I thought I meant more to him. I figured it might be a few days before I heard from him, but when it turned to weeks, I had to reach out to him through the media because I had to apologize.

The final strike to my heart was when he resurfaced in the public eye and didn't make an attempt to contact me. That was when I began to doubt if what we shared was even real.

"He still hasn't called you?" Darcy asks when she notices my sudden silence.

My lips pull into a tight line. "No."

She grabs my hand. "If he's as smart as you say, then he will, because he would be stupid to let someone as great as you slip through his fingers."

"Thank you," I whisper and squeeze her hand. "Sometimes it's easy to give up hope that he ever really loved me."

The rest of the day I busy myself taking orders and serving up some of the best burgers that New York has to offer. Flows is a block away from Times Square, so we're always hopping and we're always open. The tourists flood in here, and we're even busier than normal since one of those food television shows featured us as having one of the best burgers in the United States. So it's easy to block out the nagging heartbreak that's always on my mind while I'm here.

"Your order is up, Iris," Jason calls from the kitchen.

I smile at the tall, good-looking cook as he slides my cheeseburger platters toward me through the opening in the wall. His magnetic blue eyes sparkle, appearing even lighter today against his dark hair and tan complexion. Jason, like most of us working here, has come to the city to make it in show business. He's got the looks to make it for sure, but his voice—that's what he's been working on polishing since I met him last year.

"Thanks, Jason." I set the plates on my tray.

"Iris, I was wondering if you'd like to go out with me and a couple friends tonight."

I frown. "Oh, I don't—"

He holds his hands up and smiles. "No pressure. I just thought you've looked sad lately and I wanted to cheer you up. You can totally bring Darcy along, and we'll go out for a late dinner and just hang out."

"Did I just hear my name?" Darcy asks as she slides up next to me and throws a flirty smile in Jason's direction.

"I was just inviting you and Iris to come hang out with me and a couple of my buddies tonight." He shoots her a heart-stopping smile and her cheeks noticeably redden.

Darcy has had a thing for Jason since our manager, Ester, hired him. Darcy will kill me if I don't agree to this so she has a chance to spend a little time with him outside of work.

"Okay, sure. Why not? It'll be fun," I say.

Jason smiles. "Awesome! Pick a place that you want to meet at tonight."

Darcy takes a couple steps back so that Jason can't see her face, and she grins and mouths "thank you" before licking her lips in a seductive way that tells me her thoughts are solely focused on our handsome chef.

That night Darcy and I meet up with Jason and his friend Shane, who is equally as attractive as Jason but has no interest in theater whatsoever. Shane's a day trader, hoping to make it big on Wall Street. I guess everyone who comes to New York really does have a dream.

Darcy leans into Jason as they sit across from me and Shane in the booth, putting on her best come-hither expressions for the guy she's been too shy to ask out directly for nearly a year but has been mad crushing on. She's in seventh heaven right now.

"So, Jason tells me you have an audition tomorrow?" Shane asks as his warm, hazel eyes focus on me, giving me his undivided attention.

Shane's cute in that uptight businessman kind of way. His face has strong, masculine features like a chiseled jawline with a nice clean shave and a perfect smile. His kind eyes are evenly spaced and placed below perfectly trimmed eyebrows. The dark hair on the top of his head is cropped short but has a bit of gel in it for style.

I take a sip of my lime margarita and nod. "Yes. It's just a small role with only a couple lines, but I'd get to join in the cast in a few songs, so I'm excited."

He grins. "Hey, everyone has to start somewhere, right? And I'm sure you'll whomp it over the fence."

I laugh at his mixed-up metaphor. "You mean knock it out of the park, don't you?"

"No." He laughs. "I hate using the same old boring lines to express things, so I tend to mix things up a little on purpose. It's just this weird thing I like to do."

"That's cute," I tell him.

"You're cute," he immediately says with hopeful eyes, and I blush. "You know, Iris, if you need some moral support for tomorrow, I would be happy to go with you."

I lift my eyebrows. "Really? Wow. That's very nice of you, but totally not necessary."

Shane nods. "A little too forward on my part, I apologize. I tend to do that sometimes too."

"It's okay." I pat his hand. "It was a kind gesture."

His eyes flit down to my hand and then back up to my face. "Maybe you'll give me another chance sometime to not screw things up with my too-forward first impressions."

Shane seems like a supersweet man, and if this would've been prior to me meeting Ace White, I might've actually been interested, but Ace has ruined me for all other men. I can't help but compare Shane now, and my heart just isn't feeling anyone who isn't Ace.

Maybe someday that will change, but for now, I just can't imagine dating anyone else.

"Perhaps, someday. I just had my heart broken, and I'm just not ready to date yet."

"I understand." Shane gives me a sad smile like he's disappointed but doesn't push me any more. "Now let's just enjoy the rest of the night and pretend like I didn't just make this awkward as hell for us."

I spend the rest of the night with my friends and my new companion, Shane, relaxing and laughing, doing my best to ignore the fact that I have an impending audition looming over me. I want to land the role so bad, and the one person I desperately want around for moral support won't be there.

"Iris Easton, you're up," the stagehand announces to the group of over fifty women that I'm up against for this role.

I nod and push myself up off the stage floor, make my way over to the center mark, and acknowledge the director and his crew, who are sitting in the first row, centered in the auditorium. "I'm Iris Easton, and I'll be auditioning for Sylvia."

"Proceed with the song choice that you've prepared for us," the director calls out.

I nod toward the pianist, and the petite woman with blond hair begins playing the notes for "I'm Not That Girl." My natural instinct is to close my eyes and sing, but all of the performance things I've worked on with Ace rush back to my mind, and I'm reminded that I need to connect with the audience instead of shutting them out like I have the habit of doing.

I take a deep breath and make eye contact with the director, lifting my head, showing him that I'm proud of my ability to sing this song. When I open my mouth, the words flow from me, and there's no faking the emotion of feeling broken. It's real, because this song reminds me so much of Ace that it physically hurts.

On the last lyric of the song, my voice wavers as I'm overcome with emotion and allow the tears to fall down my cheeks.

I sniff and wipe my face just as the director says, "Okay, we'll be in touch. Next."

I clutch my chest as I walk off stage, knowing that even if I don't land this part, I put every bit of emotion I had into it and left my heart lying out there on the floor. I have no regrets about what I just did out there.

I close my eyes, wishing that I could pick up the phone and call Gran or be able to run into Ace's arms and tell him how well that went, but I can't. Both of them are gone out of my life, and I'm all alone.

After I'm only about five blocks from the theater, I spot a familiar face passing by me on the street. "Shane?"

Today he's dressed in a fitted black suit and gray tie, looking pretty hot in his business attire.

He smiles the moment his hazel eyes meet mine. "Iris? Hi. How are you? Did you have your audition yet?"

I return his smile with one of my own, flattered that he remembered. "Yes. I just came from there, actually."

"How'd it go?" he asks with genuine interest shining in his expression.

I shrug. "I won't know for a week or so if I get a callback, but I feel like I did my best."

Shane nods. "That's all anyone can ever ask for, right?"

It's hard not to get caught up in his positivity. I can't stop smiling at him. His happiness is infectious. "So what brings you out this way?"

He motions to the restaurant behind him. "I had lunch with a friend and I was about to catch a cab back to work; do you want to share one?"

I shake my head. "I'm heading home to Brooklyn. That's completely out of your way."

"I don't mind," he answers instantly with an easy smile on his face. "I'll happily ride in the back of a cab around the city if that means I get to talk to you more."

Heat floods my cheeks and I know without a doubt I'm blushing fiercely. I chew on my bottom lip while I gaze up at Shane's hopeful expression. He's a really nice guy—maybe the nicest man I've ever met in this city. I want to give him a chance but I'm not ready to date. I am, however, ready for a friend.

"If I say yes, can this just be as friends?" I ask, hopeful that this doesn't offend him.

His lips pull into a smile. "I would love to be your friend."

Twenty minutes later the cab pulls up to a stop on my curb and I push my door open. Shane slides out behind me, asking the cabbie to please wait for a moment.

He turns to me. "Iris, I'd really like to see you again. I know you've been hurt, and when you're ready to date again, please call me?"

I nod. "I will."

"Great. Oh, and congratulations on doing well on your audition. Let me know if you get the part. I'd love to watch you perform."

I place my hand on his forearm and give it a slight squeeze. "Thank you."

Touching him wasn't exactly meant to be an invitation, but Shane seizes the opportunity to place a light kiss on my cheek. He bites his lip as he pulls back with a bashful expression. "Congratulations . . . again. I know you've landed the part, and I can't wait to watch you perform on opening night."

I blush and tuck a loose strand of hair behind my ear. "I'd love for you to be there. It would be nice to have a friendly face in the audience."

"Then you can count on it. See you around, Iris," Shane says before he slips back into the cab.

I watch with my arms wrapped around me as the cab weaves in and out of traffic, eventually disappearing out of sight.

Things would be so much easier if I could just talk to Ace. Maybe if I had closure on our relationship, I could move on with a nice guy like Shane.

ACE

I clear my throat as the phone rings three times before a familiar voice on the other side of the country answers. "Hello?"

"Adele, it's Ace," I reply, letting her know who it is so she doesn't instantly hang up on me.

"Boy . . . where have you been? I thought you were a smart one. Why are you screwing up so bad?"

I shake my head. In the little time that I got to know Adele, I quickly learned that she isn't one to beat around the bush, so I've learned to be the same way with her in return. "I know, but I'm ready to fix it. I've got all my issues sorted now, and I think I'm able to handle seeing her without the media circus following behind me. We need to talk without a million eyes watching us. Will you tell me where to find her?"

"Pssssh. I shouldn't tell you, seeing as how Iris went on national television to reach out to you. The girl poured her heart out. You should've called her, even if it was to tell her it was over between the two of you."

It's like Adele to just shoot an arrow into the center of my chest, making me feel like the biggest fucking asshole in existence, but I had my reasons. "Iris was the one who told me to leave. She was the one who said that she didn't want me anymore—that she was afraid of me. Leaving and cutting all contact with her was the wrong thing to do, I know that now. I should've stayed. I should've made her see that I would do anything to protect her, but I needed to give what happened between us space."

"I think she might've been worried that you couldn't control your temper, but you could've proved to her that you could. I mean, hell, she fell in love with you, didn't she? She must've seen the caring side of you too, and I'm sure that far outweighs everything else. She told you to leave to protect you. I suppose all she was trying to do was save you from getting discovered. Why didn't you call her and let her explain all that, then you all could've worked everything else out?"

There are so many things I wish I could've handled differently. Sometimes I think if I would've just stayed put and refused to leave her side, things between us would be so much better right now. I could've proved myself to her—made her comfortable with me—but running again has only screwed things up more.

I jam a hand into my hair and drop my head into my hand as I hold the phone to my ear. "I was scared that she didn't love me anymore. I wasn't sure if what she said on television was true or not, and it fucked with my head. At the time I had a lot of shit that I still needed to deal with. I was still running from everything, including Iris, but since the day I left, I've done nothing but think of her. It's been hell without her, but I had to get clearheaded before I was ready to see her. I need to see her—hear what she has to say, even if it's not the things I want to hear. Over the phone won't work because I can't look into her eyes while she answers if she still loves me. I have to be able to see her face in order to know if we can work all this out."

Adele sighs into the phone. "And you say you've gotten yourself all straightened out now?"

"Yes," I answer without any reservation.

"If I give you her information and you hurt her again, boy, I'll take my first trip out of this state in thirty years to come to California and whip your butt. So promise me that you'll do right by her, and I'll give it to you."

"You have nothing to worry about, Adele. I swear to you that I won't break her heart again if she'll give me a chance to win it back."

"Don't make me regret this," she says before she fires off Iris's address in New York.

Two days later I find myself sitting in a parked Lincoln Town Car outside the address Adele gave me for Iris in New York. I'm not sure how long I've sat here—three hours, maybe—and I'm sure the driver is fed up with my refusal to leave this spot, but I have to see her. It's been over five weeks since I've seen her, and I don't think I can wait much longer.

Adele told me Iris had an audition today, so I've been camped out here waiting for her to return, watching every single person that's come or gone into the building.

The anticipation is killing me.

Just as I'm ready to lay my head back and give my eyes a break from constant people watching, I spot her.

I jump out of the car, leaving the door wide open in my haste to get to her, but halt in my tracks when I notice that she's not getting out of the cab alone.

My breath catches when my eyes land on Iris standing there, talking with a man in a suit that she obviously knows somehow. They speak intimately, and my pulse throbs under every inch of my skin like I'm about to explode because of seeing her with another man. But my worst fear of Iris no longer wanting me raises its ugly head the moment she lays her hand on his forearm and he leans in and kisses her cheek. My entire fucking world stops as I clutch my chest while my heart crumbles into a million pieces.

Maybe I am too late. I was a fucking idiot to ever believe that someone as amazing as Iris would be just sitting around pining for me while I got my shit together and ignored her every attempt to reach me. She hasn't called my number in weeks. I couldn't bring myself to answer her. I was scared, and that's a shitty excuse, but I wasn't sure how much damage I'd done to us by ignoring her the way I did.

A tear slips down my cheek as I realize it might be best if I just leave her alone.

She waves good-bye to the man in the cab, and instantly I know without a doubt this man means something to her. Is he her boyfriend? Did he profess his love to her? Does he touch her—caress her? It's not fucking fair, because that should've been me, not that suit-wearing douche bag she was just with. There's no way he's as passionate about her as I am.

I shove my hand into my hair as my shoulders slump and I drop my head. It's over. I can't fucking believe it's over. I've been holding on to hope that she was waiting for me even though I've been a huge asshole and not reached out. The possibility has weighed on my mind that she might move on if I didn't come to her someday soon—but I didn't think she'd be with another guy already. Am I that fucking easy to get over?

I scrub my hands down my face, wiping away the moisture from my eyes in the process, before I allow myself one last look at her before

I go. She's just as beautiful as I remembered, with her dark hair spilling down her back while her cheeks flush a rosy red. I don't know if I'll ever be able to get over Iris Easton, but it's clear to me now that I'll have to find a way to move on, because she clearly has.

I grip the handle of the door as I slip back into the car and close myself inside.

"Driver, please head back to JFK Airport," I order and close my eyes as the car passes her by, but I dare not take another look, because I don't think my heart can take it.

IRIS

A blaring horn on the busy New York street draws my attention the minute Shane's cab is out of sight. It's typical to hear drivers expressing road rage all the time in this city, so I'm not sure why I even bother looking, but something else immediately catches my eye.

There in the middle of the busy sidewalk is Ace, getting into a black town car right outside my apartment door.

"Ace!" I scream, but there's too much noise for him to hear me, so I try again. "Ace!"

I break out into a full sprint toward him, but the door closes and the car pulls away from the curb.

Why is he leaving? Doesn't he see that I'm right here, screaming his name, chasing after him—needing him?

The car slips into the busy street, and I dart through the parked cars just in time to watch it pass me without so much as a tap of the brakes.

When the car is out of reach, I stop running and stand in the street. Horns blare all around me as the cabbies curse at me to get out of the way, but I can't make myself move, knowing the man I love is running away from me yet again. Why would he come here and then leave without seeing me?

Then it hits me. He *did* see me . . . and I'm sure he's thinking the worst about Shane kissing me. It's not what he thinks.

My legs wobble as all the anger, sadness, and guilt overwhelm me at once. I need to talk to him and explain. He needs to know that this thing between us isn't over for me.

I fish my cell out of my back pocket and dial his number. On the forth ring it goes directly into a voice mail without a greeting. "Ace, I know you saw me. It's not what you think. Come back. Let's talk. Let me explain. Call me, please."

It's a long shot to call him, because he's never answered any of my other calls, but I have to at least try. I need to put the ball back in his court. Now all I can do is continue to wait.

28

IRIS

Ms. Easton?" the male voice on the other end of my cell asks.

"Yes, this is Iris," I reply, wondering who the man is, because the voice I don't recognize at all.

"This is Mark Talsman. I'm directing *Forgiving Lesley*, and I would like to have you come back in and read for me. I know you auditioned for Sylvia, but I want you to read for the lead role of Lesley."

My mouth drops open and I gasp. It's been nearly two weeks since I auditioned for that play. I just figured that I didn't get it, so this call is like a dream. My very first callback from a director, and he's offering to allow me to read for the *starring* role on a new Broadway play? What planet is this?

"Are you there?" Mr. Talsman asks.

"Yes! Yes, I'm here, and yes, I would love to read for the role of Lesley," I answer, unable to contain my giddiness.

He chuckles slightly. "Great. Be back at the theater at ten sharp, and make sure you bring that same moving performance with you."

"Yes sir. I will. Thank you so much."

After I thank him again, he ends the call and I find myself twirling like a lunatic in the middle of a busy Manhattan sidewalk.

I can't believe it. My dream—it's actually happening.

I burst into tears, heartbroken that I can't thank Ace in person for coming into my life, shaking the shit out of things, and making me a better performer. I owe him my gratitude, even if he doesn't want anything to do with me anymore.

Not knowing how else to reach him, I search for the only number I have to connect with him and dial it. I haven't tried this number in two weeks—not since the day I saw him driving away from me. I used to call it daily, but every single one of my attempts went unanswered. It will probably be no different today, I just need to hear his voice. I want to share my fantastic news with him.

The number rings and the automated voice comes on the line. The message I leave isn't too long, not too short, but I hope he actually listens to it, because God, I miss him so much.

I pause, not knowing what else I can say, so I simply hang up. A tear leaks down my cheek. There're so many emotions flowing through me: hurt, pain, anger, but most of all overwhelming sadness for the loss of the relationship I had with him. I thought I meant more to him. I would think what we had would at least warrant a phone call to tell me that he never wants to see me again if that's how he truly feels, and above all else, I wonder what he came to say to me at my apartment that day but never got the chance to.

I quickly dial the next person I can't wait to share the news with.

"What's up, Dancing Queen?" Birdie asks excitedly before she even mutters a hello.

"I'm fabulous," I say with a dreamy sigh.

"Okay, out with it. I'm on pins and needles here waiting. Did you get a callback from your last audition?"

"Yes!" I squeal. "But that's not the best part."

"What could be any better than that? Isn't that what you've been dreaming of—finally landing a role on Broadway?" she asks, and my heart pounds ninety miles a minute.

"I got a callback for the lead role." Even I can hear the excitement in my voice as I tell her my news.

"Shut the fuck up!" She giggles, clearly delighted. "The lead. Wow! Congratulations, Iris. That's great news! When do you go back to read for that part?"

"Tomorrow morning. I'm nervous as hell," I admit. "I wish you were here for moral support."

"Aw, me too. I would be there if I could, you know that. It's just hard to walk away from my job at Angel's. Tips are really adding up, and I can't miss out on the cash. Me and Grandma need it, you know." I can tell she's frowning, and I want to let her off the hook by showing her I understand.

"Well, you can make it up to me. If I get the role, then I'll pay for you and Adele to fly up and watch the show on opening night. Deal?" I ask.

"You might as well book our tickets then, because I know you'll get it." There's no waver or teasing in her voice. "You got this, Iris. You were born to shine on Broadway."

I smile, loving the fact that through all the ups and downs in my life, Birdie has always been there for me. She's more like a sister than my best friend, and I love her to pieces. She and Adele are the only people I have left in my life who truly love me back.

"Thanks. That means a lot," I tell her. "I miss you so much."

"Oh, no. I know that pouty tone. You called him again, didn't you?"

I roll my eyes. Sometimes it's scary how well she knows me.

I sigh. "I did, but only to tell him the news. I felt like I owed a call to him since he helped me so much with my singing."

"He's an idiot," Birdie mutters, and I can tell she's scowling. "One day he'll wake up and kick himself for being a jackass for letting you go."

"I pushed him away, remember?" I remind her.

"True, but you also left fifty messages apologizing before I threatened you with violence if you called him again. He had ample opportunity to come back to you. It's his own fault for showing up after five weeks of silence and seeing a man being nice to you. If he's that much of a jackhole that he won't even let you explain what he saw, then he doesn't deserve you. That's why from this point on, I'm forbidding you from ever calling him again if you don't want me to personally fly to New York just to kick your cute little ass."

"All right. All right." I laugh but know she means business.

"Good, now repeat after me: I, Iris Easton."

"Birdie . . ." I complain.

"Just do it," she orders.

I roll my eyes, feeling really silly, but go along with her because I know she won't drop it until I do. "I, Iris Easton."

"Promise to never call the douche canoe ever again," she says with an authoritative tone to her voice.

I mutter the words but don't really mean it, because when it comes to Ace, I can't seem to control my actions.

"Feel better?" Birdie's voice turns cheery.

"No," I laugh. "But do I at least get an A for effort?"

"You're impossible," she laughs. "Call me tomorrow and tell me all about the callback. I'm so excited." There's a rustling on her end of the line. "I just hugged myself and pretended I was giving you a hug for luck, even though you won't need it. You're going to blow them away tomorrow. I have faith."

After she hangs up, I still find myself thinking about Ace. Birdie's right. I have to stop begging him to give me another chance. It's been two weeks since he was here and saw me and Shane together, so maybe it's time to give up hope and move on. I just wish my heart would listen to my logical brain.

ACE

I haven't left my house in nearly two weeks. Jane Ann has limited herself to only contacting me by phone or text since the last time she was here, when she told me I was a disgusting mess who needed to shower.

She's right. I should at least shower, but I don't even have the energy for that.

The thought of Iris being with another man guts me to the point that I can hardly go on.

She left me a message after I saw her that day. She wanted to explain herself, but I know what I saw. There was something going on between her and the suit-wearing douche bag, and I can't call her back and listen to her lie to me, trying to convince me that there isn't. I'm not stupid.

I would give anything to know how she's doing—to know if

she's happy—but I've forced myself to stay away. She's obviously moved on, and I can't go on trying to get her back into my life if she doesn't want to be here. That doesn't stop me from still obsessing about her, though.

I grab the prepaid cell phone that I used while I was on the lam and go to my voice mail box, where I've saved all the messages from when Iris attempted to contact me in the past. I haven't allowed myself to listen to them since the day I saw her, but now, thinking about her, I just need to hear her voice.

I press play and close my eyes as her voice wafts through the receiver.

When I get to the last message, I raise my eyebrows, because it's been awhile since I played these, and it surprises me that there's a new one from today.

I sit up and replay the message again, listening closely. "Ace, hi, it's Iris. I know you probably don't want to hear from me, but I wanted to let you know that I had an amazing audition thanks to the things you taught me about performing. I got a callback, and instead of the small role I initially went after, I'm going back to read for the lead role in *Forgiving Lesley*. So, I just wanted to tell you thank you and that I haven't forgotten about the money I owe you for the taxes. I've got some saved and would love for you to call me back and tell me where to send it."

An overwhelming energy runs through me to speak with Iris, but I know that probably isn't a good idea. Instead I pick up a pen and the notepad in front of me and begin working on a song that expresses every emotion that I'm feeling as I think of Iris.

In less than an hour, I stare at the lyrics before me and smile. This might just be the best damn song I've ever written, and I need to get into the studio to record it.

Chapter 30

IRIS

Darcy and Jason were both over-the-moon excited for me when I first told them about the phone call from Mark Talsman after I got to work yesterday. Instead of being attentive to the restaurant patrons, we spend most of the shift last night going over my audition piece. They even went as far as making me promise that when I become a star someday that I won't forget about them and will help them break into the business too. I laughed and told them that I would. They're my friends. Of course I'll help them if I have the opportunity. I just pray that today goes well and I get the part.

I take a deep breath and head into the auditorium. Unlike every other audition I've been to, there aren't bodies lined as far as the eye can see, all of them usually vying for the same exact parts. Today there only a few women and men standing together on the stage. It feels much more intimate this time. It's almost as if I can feel every eye in the place judging me, hoping that I'll screw up and makes their odds better for getting a role.

The same director that sat out in the auditorium the last time I was here now walks on stage in front of the group of people I'm standing with. "Good morning, everyone. I'm Mark Talsman, the director, and we called those of you in this room back because we saw something special in you when you last performed for us. My assistant, Sheila"—Mr. Talsman gestures over to the chunky woman with short, black, curly hair who is wearing a headset and holding a clipboard—"will now put you into groups based on the role you are trying out for. This is your one last shot to impress me. Put your best foot forward and pour your heart into the music. Show me what you've got. Sheila, if you will."

Sheila steps in front of us. "When I announce the role you were called for, I want you to come forward. Let's start with the leading male role of Jonah."

Four of the men in the group step in front of the rest of us, and Sheila motions them to the right of the stage. "Great. You all stay there. Next is the leading female role of Lesley." My heart races as I step out, along with only one other woman. "You two stand next to my Jonahs."

I step over to the woman who is going out for the same part as me, and can't help noticing how absolutely stunning she is. Her dark hair flows down her back and has a glorious natural shine to it. Her blue eyes pop against her tanned, toned skin, and I suddenly feel very plain next to this beauty.

After everyone is grouped up, Sheila sends our groups to different sections of the theater to sit in the rows of chairs so we can watch all the performances while we await our turns.

MICHELLE A. VALENTINE

The Jonahs are up first. One by one I observe each of their performances and take mental notes on what each one of them does right or does wrong so it can help me in my future auditions.

While they are all impressive, the last man who walks on stage blows me away with the silky tone to his voice that accompanies his model good looks. I swear all the women within earshot of me actually swooned a little, judging from their sighs.

There's really no question on who will be getting that part.

Sheila steps on stage and calls, "Veronica Constance for the part of Lesley."

The raven-haired beauty next to me stands and makes her way to the stage, and just when she opens her mouth I wonder what I'm even doing here. She's obviously got the part. She's too good not to.

Her voice flows like butter through the entire auditorium, and she projects so loudly that I'm sure her voice actually vibrates the bones of every person in the room.

I sink down in my chair and debate just throwing up the white flag and leaving, but I know that's completely unprofessional, so I decide to stick it out and see what I can learn from it.

When she's finished, Veronica actually curtsies to Mr. Talsman and walks off stage.

Sheila steps back out and calls, "Iris Easton."

I swallow hard, then lick my suddenly dry lips. My heart pounds a mile a minute as I take center stage and the same music begins to play that Veronica just sang to for the part of Lesley. Nerves shoot through me, and I take a deep breath, attempting to relax. I allow myself to close my eyes for a brief moment just to picture Ace's encouraging face. When I open them, I use his image as my motivation when singing this song about a man breaking a woman's heart. Tipping my chin up, facing Mr. Talsman, I sing my heart out.

Every single person who I consider a friend is out with me tonight as we celebrate the call I received last week from Mr. Talsman giving me the lead role in *Forgiving Lesley*. Birdie insisted on hopping a flight to come celebrate with me, and I'm glad she did. This is by far one of the most important things that can happen for my career, and it means a lot to me that she's here.

"To Iris," Shane announces, and we hold up the shots our bartender just made for us. "May she knock 'em dead and whomp it over the fence!"

I giggle at Shane and the funny way he likes to twist around old expressions.

"To Iris," Darcy, Jason, and Birdie say in unison before we all tip the amber shots back at the same time.

My lips pucker as the alcohol burns my throat on its way down to my stomach. I haven't drunk hard liquor since the last time I got completely shitfaced and Ace was there being a gentleman, taking care of me.

I sigh at even the mere thought of him.

"You didn't tell me that Shane was such a hottie," Birdie whispers in my ear.

Heat creeps up my neck and into my face, surely breaking my skin into a bright red blush. "I told you he was cute."

Birdie giggles as her eyes roam over Shane. "Cute is much different than hot. Cute is the word you use when a guy is average looking with maybe one nice feature. It's not the word you use to describe a man that's nearly full-on perfection like Shane. If I were you, I'd be all over that and be muttering 'Ace who?'"

I give her a pointed look. "I haven't mentioned Ace in a while, have I? You made me take the no-calling-the-douche-canoe oath, remember? I'm not about to call him and endure your ass-kicking wrath."

Birdie lifts one eyebrow. "You might not've called him, but it doesn't mean you still aren't sitting around pining away for him. I know you, Iris. I know you have a hard time moving on when your heart gets broken. I'm not telling you to run off with Shane and have little hot suit-wearing minibabies, but I don't see the harm in giving him a shot. He's obviously so into you."

I stare at Shane, and I totally get where Birdie is coming from. Shane is hot . . . some may even call him downright sexy with his strong jawline, dazzling smile, and the noticeably chiseled body lurking under that dress shirt. Couple all that with intriguing hazel eyes and hair . . . I can definitely see why Birdie's making a fuss because I'm not all over the man. It's hard to make her understand that the vast amount of love I still have for Ace practically blinds me to all other men.

"I'm just not ready," I confide in my best friend. "I just need a little more time. Shane understands that."

Almost as if Shane can sense that we're talking about him, he turns in my direction and smiles. His dimples *are* amazingly cute, and maybe someday I will be ready for something more with him. I lift up my drink and mouth "Thank you" to him before I turn around on the stool to watch the TV hanging over the bar, because I don't want to send off a bunch of flirty signals by just staring at him.

I raise the beer to my lips to take a sip, but my arm pauses midway. There on the screen, sitting down for another interview with Linda Bronson, is Ace.

I grab Birdie's arm and squeeze, causing her to turn around and check out what's got me so worked up.

"Oh, shit," she mutters beside me before asking the bartender to turn the volume on the television up.

Linda sits across from Ace and smiles at him. "You look well. How are things now that you've been back with your band for the last month?"

Ace rakes his hand through his bronze hair like the question makes him nervous. "It's still a work in progress, but things are getting better. We've actually been back in the studio the last couple of weeks, recording; things are really starting to come together in that department."

Linda nods and then follows up with another question. "Are these new songs going in the new direction you were telling me about last time we spoke?"

He licks his plump lips and memories flood my brain of what he tasted like on my tongue. "Yes. I've written most of the songs for the new album. There's one in particular that I'm really proud of. It's called 'Juliet, Forgive Me.'"

"That sounds like an interesting title. Does it have a meaning?"

He stiffens a bit and then nods. "It does. It's my vision of what Romeo's makeup song to Juliet might sound like if he had the opportunity to tell her he's sorry."

She grins. "Are you a fan of the classic Shakespearean works?"

"Very much so. Shakespeare is something very personal for me," Ace answers. "Same goes for the new songs."

Linda raises her eyebrows, and I can see the wheels turning in her brain as she begins digging a little deeper into what he means by that. "Did you write these songs with any particular person in mind?"

Ace tilts his head and rubs his index finger across the bottom of his chin. "I did, and she knows exactly who she is. I've got a lot of making up to do to this person, so I thought I'd start by telling her how sorry I am through a song."

I gasp and then cover my mouth with my hand. Tears well up in my eyes, and it's taking everything in me not to break down in front of all these people.

"When do you plan on releasing this song?" Linda asks.

He shrugs. "I'm not really sure. The label has control of all that, but I'm able to sing it now, if you'd like."

The camera focuses on Linda, who looks straight into the lens like she's speaking with her audience. "Wow. A new song debut right here on *Celebrity Pop Buzz Nightly*. This is a first for us." She turns her attention back to Ace as someone from the side of the shot hands him a guitar. "Viewers are in for a treat, and I hope the young lady you wrote this for is watching. Ace, whenever you're ready."

Silence falls over the television for a few moments, and then the sound of Ace strumming the acoustic guitar strings come through the speakers, followed by Ace's smooth, silky voice.

As the words flow from his mouth, he stares directly into the camera, and it's almost as if he's singing right to me. The song is about a tragic love story ending on a bad note and two people working hard to find a way to get back into each other's good graces but screwing it up every time they try to fix it. He's apologizing through the lyrics for meeting me at the wrong time and putting me through all the shit that's gone on between us since He rode into my life, but those aren't the things that strike me the most.

When he breaks into the chorus, he calls me his Juliet and calls himself the worst Romeo in history, but he wants to figure out how to be the best. He's asking me to forgive him.

Tears flow down my cheeks, and I can feel the stare of every single one of my friends watching me as I stare at the man that I love, but can seem to never have, on the screen in front of me. I'm not sure what this even means for us, but I'm praying it's a sign that he's finally coming to me.

When the song ends, Linda thanks Ace for the moving performance and wishes him well with the new album before signing off, allowing the show to cut to a commercial.

Shane's beside me, nudging his shoulder into mine, trying to cheer me up.

I swat away the tears and then sniff before acknowledging him. "Hey."

"Hey," he replies and then sighs. "I never stood a chance with you, did I?"

I glance over in his direction and see the sadness written all over Shane's face. It sucks that he's hurt, but I'm glad I never promised him anything other than friendship or I would've stomped all over his heart with this display of affection for another man.

I pull my lips into a tight line and shake my head. "That's why I couldn't give you more than friendship. I still love him."

Shane forces a smile. "It appears that he still loves you too."

Opening night has finally arrived. I've prepared for this moment for the last two months, and I'm finally ready to make my debut as Lesley, lead actress in *Forgiving Lesley*. I still can't get over my name on the marquee outside.

Me. On Broadway. I can't fucking believe it!

A text from Birdie chirps on my cell, telling me that she and Adele found their seats. I smile, loving the fact that people who love me are sitting out in that audience. I managed to get tickets for Darcy, Jason, and Shane too. They've all been there with me through my grueling rehearsal schedule and trying to keep my mind off the fact that Ace still hasn't called me despite the nationally televised serenade.

There were so many times that I wanted to quit this play because I doubted that I had what it takes to perform in the big leagues, but all my friends were right there behind me, reminding me that I was born to do this.

"Iris, it's showtime. You ready for this?" says Jacob Terrey, the beautiful man who earned the role opposite me as Jonah, Lesley's love interest—a man who I've had to practice kissing over and over for the past two months.

I smile, trying hard not to sweat. "Yes. I am so excited, nervous, but mostly excited."

Jacob wraps his arms around me and pulls me into his warm embrace. "You're going to knock them dead."

It feels nice to be hugged like this, and I'm sure to people who don't know any better, it might look like there's something going on between me and Jacob, but I'm sure his *boyfriend* would quickly correct any false assumptions.

"Thank you, Jacob. Good luck out there tonight," I tell him before he pulls away and tells me good-bye so he can go off to warm up.

Before I know it, the opening music plays, and Jacob and I, along with the rest of the cast, are out there allowing our souls to bleed before the sold-out crowd. At first, I'll admit, I am a little stiff, but I quickly loosen up and just have fun with it, making my voice that much more fluid.

I don't remember ever feeling this confident in my abilities as a performer as I do in the final moments of the play. I sing the last note, and the crowd jumps to their feet, and the theater rumbles with applause.

When the curtain comes down, Jacob and I go out holding hands to take our final bows. Adele smiles as she and Birdie stand and clap along with the rest of my friends. My feet stumble below me as I bow in my over-the-top ball gown that I wear for the final scene.

"You okay there, Iris?" Jacob asks as he tightens his hold on my hand, keeping me from falling.

"Yes, I'm good," I answer as I walk carefully off the stage.

I make it back to my dressing mirror and smile at all the beautiful flower arrangements waiting for me.

"Wow. They love you," Jacob says as he passes by and sees my display, and then he turns his attention behind me. "And it looks like they're still coming in."

I turn to a young delivery man wearing a red jacket and baseball cap who is holding a huge white box. "Ms. Easton, I've got a delivery for you." He smiles while thrusting a delivery slip toward me. "Just sign on the *X*."

I do as he instructs, writing my name carefully on the form, and then take the box. "Do you know who they're from?"

He shakes his head. "Nope, I'm sorry. I just deliver them."

"Thank you." I smile, and he nods politely and then turns on his heel and heads out the door.

I place the box down on my dressing room table and carefully untie the large red ribbon holding the box shut before lifting the lid off. Twelve breathtaking long-stem roses greet me with an amazing floral scent, and I gasp. I search for a card so I know who to thank for such a beautiful gift and find it stuffed between two of the flowers.

"To thine own self be true."

My hand flies to my mouth as I suck in a ragged breath. All this time has gone by and I've not heard a single word from him, now this? On opening night? How dare he keep toying with me like this! What do these flowers even mean? Is he sorry? Is he here?

What in the hell is going on?

Tears slip down my cheeks, and I quickly bat them away, trying hard to save my stage makeup from running and turning me into a complete mess, but it's no use. I can no longer hold back the pain that I feel, and I'm sick and tired of Ace Johnson—White—*whoever* and the hell he is playing with my emotions. I've waited long enough. It's time I track him down and demand some answers.

My chest rises and falls at such an accelerated speed that I'm going to hyperventilate if I can't calm down. I wish he was here. I need to yell at him—scream at the top of my lungs to get out weeks of pure frustration.

"Damn," Jacob teases. "I've never seen anyone develop a pure expression of dismay over getting flowers. Usually they conjure the opposite emotion."

I throw the card back in the box and shake my head. "I know . . . it's just these flowers . . . well, the sender, rather, confuses the shit out of me. He hasn't spoken to me in so long . . . I don't understand why he keeps playing with me like this. I don't like being strung along."

He nods. "Men are dumbasses sometimes. Take it from me. I am one. But I'm sure, whoever he is, that he'll get his head out of his ass. He'd be stupid to lose you. Hell, if I was a straight man, I would steal you away myself."

I shake my head and laugh. "You are too much, but thank you."

Jacob wraps one hand around my shoulders and pulls me into a friendly hug. "You're welcome, gorgeous. Try not to be so down. You did amazing out there. Don't let an asshole keep you from enjoying yourself tonight."

After Jacob leaves me alone at my dressing table, I find myself just staring at the box of roses, wondering about Ace. While I'm still angry with him, I still want him. I just don't understand why he hasn't called me. There are so many things that could be worked out between us if he would only give me a chance to explain about what he saw with Shane.

My shoulders slump, and the fire I felt when I first received the flowers morphs into the typical sadness that fills me whenever I allow myself to think about how much I miss Ace.

Everyone for the past few weeks has encouraged me to move on when he didn't immediately contact me after singing that song on *Celebrity Pop Buzz Nightly*. I thought for sure he'd want to make up with me after that, but I heard nothing, and that hurt the worst. It made me feel like I meant nothing at all to him. So my friends are all probably right. I need to stop holding on to hope that Ace and I will ever get back together.

My cell buzzes inside my purse with an incoming call. I grab my bag from under the dressing table and fish out my phone before I answer, "What's up, Birdie?"

"Hey!" she yells into the phone while a crowd mumbles around her. "We're all out in front of the theater. How much longer will you be? We're waiting to celebrate with you."

I glance up at my reflection in the mirror and sigh. "I still have my costume on and all the stage makeup, so it'll take me some time to get all that off. There's a little bar and grill a couple blocks away called Sunny's Place. If you all want to wait on me there, I'll be down as soon as I get all this crap off."

"Okay," she answers. "I'll see you in a bit."

I tell my best friend good-bye and then toss my phone back into my purse before I turn my attention to the mirror and begin removing the fifty million pins from my hair.

Stagehands rush back and forth all around me, collecting and organizing all the props for tomorrow's show. There's a buzz of excitement in the air, and we all know that we're a part of something special. Everywhere I look, there are smiles, including on the face of our director, Mark. It takes a lot to impress him, so it's a great feeling knowing that our production has pleased him.

Mark has been on Broadway for a long time. His graying hair and stoic features give off the appearance of experience. I've learned so much from him over the last few weeks, and I'm so grateful that he took a chance on casting an unknown like me.

When he notices me watching him in the mirror, Mark makes his way over to me with his assistant, Shelia, in tow. Over the last few weeks of rehearsal, things have become a little more relaxed around here. Instead of Mr. Talsman, he insists we are all on a first-name basis so we bond as a unit, making everyone more comfortable.

"Iris, can I have a moment?" he asks.

"Sure." I throw the pin on the table and turn to face him.

He smiles. "The performance you just gave ranks up there with some of the best I've ever seen in my twenty years on Broadway."

Heat floods my cheeks and I can't fight the grin that stretches across my face. "Really?"

He nods. "I really mean that, and I'm sure once the reviews start popping up about the show, other directors will come knocking on your door. I have a feeling that you're bound for great things."

"Mark, your car is here," Shelia says as she continues to glance down at her phone.

"Okay," he says to her before turning back in my direction. "Congratulations, Iris. I'll see you for tomorrow's performance."

I fight the urge to squeal like a twelve-year-old girl who has just found out her crush likes her back. That's the nicest thing Mark's ever said to me, and it's boosted my confidence in myself tenfold.

Still floating on cloud nine after I remove all my stage gear, I push through the side door of the theater smiling. I take a deep breath of the crisp evening New York air, and then it instantly whooshes from my lungs the moment I spot a familiar face.

There, standing on the sidewalk, is Ace in a black leather jacket and faded blue jeans. He's just as sexy as I remember, and that pisses me off. It makes it a whole lot harder to hate him when he looks so good, but that's not going to stop me from giving him a piece of my mind.

My eyes drift down to the single red rose he's holding in his hands before they focus on the hopeful expression he's wearing. Does he honestly think sending me flowers and showing up here on the most important night of my life automatically earns his way back into my good graces?

Gah! This is unbelievable.

I shake my head. "What are you doing here?"

He licks his lips slowly, and damn it, I wish I could say the action disgusts me, but it does just the opposite. It makes me miss his mouth and the crazy way it made me feel when he used to put it on me.

"I came to see you." He takes a step toward me and holds out the flower. "This is for you."

I pull my lips into a tight line but refuse to take it from him.

He frowns after I make it obvious that I'm not going to make his apology easy. He hurt me and I don't know if I can forgive him for it.

He pulls his hand back, taking the rose with it. "Did you get the others?"

I sigh. "I did. Thank you."

It's the lamest show of gratitude I've ever made, but it's impossible to fake being happy over receiving them, especially since my initial reaction to them was anger.

His hand holding the rose falls limply to his side and he shoves his other hand into his hair. "This isn't going anything like I envisioned."

It's almost as if he only meant to think that last statement instead of saying it aloud, because his eyes snap to mine the moment I fire back, "What exactly did you expect, Ace? Did you think that just because you decide to acknowledge my presence again that I would just be so glad that you've finally come to me that I'd just jump right into your arms? No fucking questions asked? Do you not know me at all?" Tears leak out of my eyes and I bat them away. "Fuck you, Ace. Just fuck you, all right. I poured my heart out to you over and over again and you didn't give a damn."

Pain flickers across his face. "That's where you're wrong. I stayed away because I did give a damn. *You* told me to leave. I was just doing what you asked me to do."

"I told you to leave to protect you!" I shout, causing a few passersby to jerk their heads in our direction. "It killed me to lie to you—to say things that hurt you, but I didn't know another way. I was hoping you'd call me out and see through my bullshit, but I understand why you ran. I didn't expect you to accept my apology easily, but it tore my heart apart when every time I reached out to you, you rejected me. Even after you sang 'Juliet, Forgive Me,' I've heard nothing from you until today. I just don't want to be hurt anymore."

This time it's him who allows the tears to fall. He stares at me like I've just punched him in the gut and left him gasping for air. I'm glad he's here to know just how pissed off I am. He deserves to see how much he's hurt me.

He stares into my eyes as he says, "I know that I fucked up, okay? I knew it the moment I got on my bike and left that it would change everything between us, but damn it, it didn't make me stop wanting you—needing to be with you. I'm sorry I hurt you, but *you* hurt me too, and I handled things all wrong by staying away."

His eyes glisten as he closes the distance between us and touches my face. "Forgive me, please. I love you and I don't want to live without you anymore. The taste of you still lingers on my lips, and no matter how much I tried to make myself forget about you, I couldn't. We were made for each other. I know staying away for so long makes that hard to believe, but it's the God's honest truth.

You've worked your way into my soul, and I'm afraid that you've etched yourself onto my heart permanently."

My heart bangs in my chest as I close my eyes to allow my brain to absorb everything he's just said. It feels so good to hear him admit that he wants me too—that he's been hurting just like I have, but even with his sweet plea for forgiveness, I still have my doubts.

"How do I know when things get hard that you won't run off again? My heart won't survive going through this kind of break again," I whisper.

"You'll have to trust me," he says. "I know that's a lot to ask, but the only way that I can prove to you that I'm never going anywhere again is for you to let me back into your life. I will never leave your side again. I swear it."

Strong fingers wrap around my waist as he pulls me into him. "Please, Iris. I'm begging you."

My eyes lock on a set of russet ones. They are the same eyes I once stared into while the man I love held me in his arms. Tears run down my cheeks and I feel my resolve wavering. I know it's a risk, but right now I can't deny that I'm in love with this man.

"You've got a lot of making up to do," I tell him with a small smile.

His eyes brighten, and he attempts to fight back a smile as he cups my face. "I'm willing to put in the work. You're worth it."

"I'm not going to make it easy, you know," I threaten, causing him to laugh.

"I would be disappointed if you did." This time his glorious grin comes at me in full force. "You were amazing tonight."

I raise my brow. "You saw the show?"

He nods. "I wouldn't have missed this for anything. You took my breath away when you sang. You were perfection."

"Kiss her already!" someone walking by on the street shouts at us, reminding me that we aren't alone in this tender reunion.

"I love you," he whispers. "Forever."

I bite my lip. "I love you too."

Ace grins and then plants his lips on mine. Instantly I melt into him, enjoying the taste of his lips while we show the world a kiss that would rival any on-screen scene and begin the sequel to our own epic romance.

ACKNOWLEDGMENTS

First off, I want to thank you, my dear readers, for giving this book a shot!

Emily Snow, Kelli Maine, and Kristen Proby (aka the Wicked Mafia), the past couple of years with you all have been amazing. Thank you for your love and support. Love you guys hard!

Jennifer Wolfel, I can never thank you enough for reading a million versions of this story and hashing out the bugs with me. Ace and Iris are so much stronger because of your love of this story and willingness to see it through to the end with me.

Toski Covey, thank you for being my first test subject on this story idea. Your input on this novel was amazing! It helped me to keep pushing forward.

Holly Malgieri, my assistant extraordinaire, thank you so much for everything you do for me and my books. Means a lot.

Jennifer Foor, thank you for being one of my most trusted friends and reminding me these books don't write themselves.

Kelsie Leverich, thank you for being my procrastination partner in crime and being there to chat about books.

Jill Marsal, thank you for being an amazing agent and believing in me and my work.

Charlotte Hescher and Deb Taber, thank you for working your

butts off on this manuscript and pushing me hard. It's so much better after you two put your touches on it.

To my awesome Montlake editors, Maria Gomez and Hai-Yen Mura, thank you for taking a chance on me.

My beautiful ladies in Valentine's Vixens Group, you all are the best. You guys always brighten my day and push me to be a better writer. Thank you!

To the romance blogging community, thank you for always supporting me and my books. I can't tell you how much every share, tweet, post, and comment means to me. I read them all, and every time I feel giddy. THANK YOU for everything you do. Blogging is not an easy job, and I can't tell you how much I appreciate what you do for indie authors like me. You totally make our world go round.

Last, but always first in my life, my husband and son: thank you for putting up with me. I love you both more than words can express.

ABOUT THE AUTHOR

Photo © 2014 Kent Smith

Michelle A. Valentine is the *New York Times* and *USA Today* bestselling author of *Rock the Heart. Wicked White* is the first novel in her Wicked White romance series. She attended college as a drafting and design major, but her love of people soon persuaded her to join the nursing field. It wasn't until after the birth of her son that she began her love affair with romance novels, and she hasn't looked back since. When she's not writing, she feeds her music addiction, dabbles in party planning, and expresses herself by working with arts and crafts. She currently lives in Columbus, Ohio, with her husband, son, and two beloved dogs.

11-15

DISCARD